LORD OF
THE KILL

THEODORE TAYLOR

LORD OF THE KILL

THE BLUE SKY PRESS

An Imprint of Scholastic Inc. • *New York*

THE BLUE SKY PRESS

Library of Congress catalog card number: 2001037829

ISBN 0-439-33725-9

10 9 8 7 6 5 4 3 2   03 04 05 06

Printed in the United States of America   37

First printing, November 2002

Designed by Kathleen Westray

FOR CHARLIE:

Enjoy! Enjoy!

IN APPRECIATION

I wish to thank Richard Farinato, of the Humane Society of the United States, for information and documentation about canned hunts; Deputy Sheriff Tom Cavallero, Sheriff's Department, Merced County, California, for joint raid information; Troy Swauger, of California Fish and Game, Sacramento, California, for joint raid procedures; Tippi Hedren, Director, Shambala Preserve, Acton, California, for tiger guidance; Federal Fish and Game Special Agents Garland Swain, Bill Talkin, and Jim Stinebough for canned-hunt information; and Robin Lepore, Solicitor's Office, Federal Fish and Game, Department of the Interior, for legal information relative to canned-hunt farms and ranches.

Theodore Taylor
June 2001

CONTENTS

A BODY

The black Ford Ranger pickup with three occupants moved along the county road moments before 3:00 A.M. and stopped at a power pole. All three men wore dark clothing. The driver stayed behind the wheel, the other two passengers got out, and one sat on the running board to strap on climbers. The motor remained running.

Getting a tool that resembled a small crowbar out of the truck bed, one of the men pulled on a pair of gloves and went up to the pole. The instrument dangled from his belt. Reaching a transformer near the top of his climb, he interrupted the flow of electricity to a grid that was about two miles square.

Quickly returning to the ground, he got back into the pickup. It headed south again, stopping at the rear vehicle gate in a steel outer-perimeter fence that enclosed a big-cat preserve. They cut the padlock on the gate. The gate was opened, and an aluminum extension ladder was extracted from the truck, along with a bundle — a human body wrapped in a green window drape.

The driver carried the ladder, and the other two men picked up the bundle. They all disappeared into the silent blackness, returning to the truck five minutes later, carrying only the ladder. The truck got under way for Los Angeles, to the north.

GENERAL
DMITRI ZUKOV

No creature on earth has the eye intensity of the Siberian tiger. At dusk or in the beam of a torch, their eyes blaze back ambient gold light. Their roars can be heard at a distance of five miles in the silent evergreen forests of our taiga. It would be a tragedy if we allow those magical fires to burn out because of poachers' guns. It is the Chinese medical trade that threatens every single tiger in the wild.

— Dr. Nikolai Voronov, Sikote-Alin Biosphere,
Terney, Siberia

Nearing six o'clock, sixteen-year-old Benjamin Jepson began his regular post-dawn inspection of the individual big cat compounds at Los Coyotes Preserve. It was mostly a check of the chain-link fences and their foot-thick concrete foundations for possible evidence of any of the eighty-two animals attempting to dig out overnight at the non-profit facility sixty miles south of Los Angeles. The entire preserve was surrounded by a fourteen-foot high steel chain-link perimeter fence, a barrier for any jumpers.

But this particular dripping, foggy morning in early June, Ben was puzzled by the deep silence of the canyon. The quiet was highly unusual. By this time there should have been a few early, tired roars. This thick silence was truly ominous.

Ben loved his post-dawn job of checking each of the twenty-eight compounds. The big cats of Los Coyotes Preserve were all discards from circuses, private zoos, or private owners. People bought them as pets only to find out that cubs soon weighed 400 pounds or more. All females at Los Coyotes that lived with males were on birth control pills. The lions lifted their heads to gaze at him momentarily, then dropped them down to the sands to go back to sleep. The tigers were the early birds, usually awake at dawn.

Compound Number One held General Dmitri Zukov, more than 800 pounds of grace and muscle, thirteen feet from the tip of his nose to the end of his tail. He slowly approached the padlocked gate and gave Ben wet wood-rasp kisses on the back of his hand.

Dimmy was the most famous Siberian tiger in the world, the most valuable on earth. Ringling Brothers had offered a half million rental for him for five years, simply for caged display; the Las Vegas Hilton wanted to lease him for twenty thousand a month for casino lobby display in a specially built "tiger setting." But Dmitri was not for sale or rent.

Dmitri and Ben had known each other six years. Ben had cuddled Dmitri when the rescued animal was about three weeks old in the taiga, the thick, snow-covered forest in Siberia's Sikote-Alin mountains. Poachers had killed his mother. Ben had gone to Russia with his father, Peter Jepson, on a *Save the Tigers* mission.

Ben walked on, still bothered by the utter silence. When he checked the four lionesses in Number Two, speaking to them softly by name, they simply stared at him. Usually one or two would approach the steel links. This time they didn't move. *Was something wrong at Los Coyotes?*

He passed Delilah, the cheetah he was planning to train to be a house cat. No sign that any of the cats had attempted to dig out.

Ben paused by the four Siberians in Number Eight. There were nine of them at Los Coyotes. Again, none of them responded.

He passed Number Ten. Dora, a coal-black leopard with pale hypnotic eyes, was often dangerous. If Ben wasn't careful, she'd leap onto his back when he entered her home. Some people called the black ones panthers, but they were really leopards. Their spots showed through their fur in bright sunlight. They always hid in the trees, where leaves and branches provided cover. Gentle Isabel, a snow leopard, was his favorite. She often whipped down off a limb and curled around his legs. He'd kneel in the sand and talk to her softly, caressing her. But today she didn't move.

He paused at Number Eleven and his five cougars.

The cougars were America's only native lions. They were also called pumas, catamounts, and mountain lions. They could out-jump any tiger or leopard, dropping unerringly from a tree sixty feet up to land on a deer's back.

Whenever Ben entered their compound, he always rubbed Max's russet head, and he always gave attention to Gypsy when she came purring up. Cougar fur felt like rabbit down. Daily human contact with the cats was necessary for the safety of the handlers. Yet today, like the other cats, the cougars were strangely silent. *What was wrong?*

Many nights, sometimes with his best friend Jilly Coombes, or his parents — when they were home — he took the same compound walks to check on the cats. Some would be pacing restlessly or sprawled out in the sand. Their moods were different when the moon was full or when the wind blew through the cottonwoods. He talked to them as he went by, calling them each by name. Their eyes, mostly coppery green-hued at night, shined at him, particularly when the night was so black as to be solid. In the full witching moon, the tigers paced and growled, as did the leopards and jaguars, making their own sounds. Day or night, these were mystical walks in a mystical place, and Ben treasured them.

Each breed of cat was so different. The restless tigers loved raw, cold winter weather and downpours. They raised their heads to the sky and closed their eyes, as if praying. They didn't move a muscle as the water pelted down. The sissy lions, hating rain, always went to bed early, entering their huts at twilight. In colder weather, Ben made certain their heat lamps were burning. Some were elderly and suffered from arthritis.

Ben went on, still feeling apprehensive. Wearing dusty high-top Uggs, naked to the waist in the high humidity of the canyon in summer, he had never been an attractive kid. His hair was natural straw blond and longish. The only thing appealing about his round, pancake face and his pug nose was a spread of freckles, but at least he had a radiant smile.

His body was hard and muscular, and he was capable of handling 500-pound cats though he was only five feet seven, weighing in at 130 pounds. Both his parents were tall and handsome — *something I'll never be*, he thought — and the fact bothered him.

But for now, he put aside all other thoughts. *Something is wrong, something is wrong.* The eerie silence was deafening.

THE BLOODY
JAGUARS

Ben finally reached Number Twelve, home of the black-spotted jaguars. They were named Pico and Iris, and they were the most vicious cats of all. They'd battle crocodiles and win. He frowned at them in the gray-silver light and had a sudden chill. Their faces appeared to be smeared with dried blood.

He went closer, and the eight-foot-long jags coughed at him in a different tone than he'd ever heard. *Where did the blood come from?* He'd never known them to fight each other. And there was no sign of injury on them.

His heart was now speeding. He slowly circled their compound.

Few humans had ever "gone in" with Pico and Iris; they seemed to have a natural hatred of humans. Their eyes tracked humans with a cold robotic intensity.

Then, behind their den house, Ben saw a pile of torn green cloth. The low fog partially obscured it. In the ripped cloth there seemed to be a half-eaten human corpse with dark stains soaked into the yellow sand beside it.

Ben sucked in a breath. He thought back to one Halloween, four years back, when some kids threw a dummy smeared with ketchup into Dmitri's space, enraging the Siberian. But Ben didn't think what was in Number Twelve was a dummy. He took a closer look and muttered, "Oh, my God." Then he was running to the Jepsons' cottage, heart now drumming with shock and fright, mind clicking away about what to do.

Inside the cottage, Ben immediately called Deputy Sheriff Harry Metcalf at home. He was still breathless when Metcalf said, "Okay, Ben, what wacko did what to you now?" Metcalf was always calm.

"I think there's a dead body in the jaguars' compound."

"Why do you think that, Ben?"

"There's blood all over the place; the jaguars have it smeared on their faces. The body looks like it's half-eaten."

"Oh, man," said Harry Metcalf. "You sure it's a body?" he added skeptically.

"I'm sure, Mr. Metcalf, and my parents are in India."

"Ouch! Let me finish breakfast, and I'll come over. Meanwhile, you stay at home. Don't go down there. If memory serves me, that compound is on the north end. Right?"

"Right."

"Keep everybody away."

"Yessir."

As the phone clicked off, Ben wondered if what had happened in Number Twelve was just another crazy "incident," the worst one ever. Or was it murder?

Ben had known for ten years that Los Coyotes drew weirdos and wackos, the nuts who wanted to challenge the big cats, taunt them. Metcalf had arrested a pink-haired fifteen-year-old for trespassing three years ago when she climbed an oak tree and crawled out on a limb, then dropped into a lioness space, sobering up fast when Doris and Opal rose to greet her. She went back up the oak, screaming. Ben's mother had rescued her. There was an old woman who spent hours outside the perimeter fence "baby talking" to Dmitri.

There'd been other incidents. One Fourth of July, an idiot had fired skyrockets into the compounds, panicking the big cats. Ever since, Ben, his father and mother, and the armed staff had patrolled the road above Los Coyotes each Fourth to prevent a repeat.

Then there'd been the attack last year by the deranged ex-Navy Seal Thomas Hedgepeth, who had shot at the animals, killing five, and then tried to burn down the preserve. But this incident was entirely different than anything in the past.

School at El Toro High had ended for the summer, and Ben had become the boss of Los Coyotes four days ago, taking over the 195 acres from Alfredo Garcia, the chief animal handler who'd been suddenly hospitalized. His father and mother, who administered the preserve, were in India to write and photograph a National Geographic story about Bengal tiger poachers who illegally killed the animals for profit. Ready or not, Ben had become the boss. But he hadn't been worried. He'd been around the big cats since he was six, and he knew more about them than any of the staffers — even Alfredo. If Ben needed help, he could call on Larry Templeton, his dad's best friend and the main preserve veterinarian. Dr. Templeton was like one of the family.

Ben left the cottage to warn Alfredo's helpers, Luis Vargas, Rafael Soto, and Enrique Castillo. He needed to tell them what had happened in Number Twelve. *Stay away from it.* He sent Luis to go tell the Kenyan, Dr. Hudson Odinga, and the Chinese student, Quan Li. They all lived in the preserve's central housing area.

When his father, founder of the preserve, was home, which hadn't been too often the past few years, he was, of course, the executive chief, master of both animals and staff.

Alfredo had awakened during the night with severe abdominal pains. He'd been bothered by them for more than a week. Ben rushed him to the nearest hospital where emergency doctors discovered he had a life-threatening ruptured appendix. They also discovered several tumors. Alfredo would be in intensive care for at least four days, out of action for at least a month.

When Ben returned to the cottage, he called Larry Templeton and Susan Trager, the preserve attorney. For the time being, and until Deputy Metcalf had examined what Ben thought was a corpse, Larry and Susan would be the essential people in his life.

Ben's father and mother were too far away to be of immediate help, but he'd try to reach them if Deputy Metcalf thought the evidence pointed to murder. Ben needed to shift Pico and Iris quickly to an unoccupied compound — an unwelcome, uneasy chore. They were both lightning fast and could leap ten feet in an eye blink with jaws wide open.

It was only 7:00, but Ben was exhausted. He made some toast and hot chocolate. Then he sat down to wait for Metcalf. Only then did he begin to think about how that body got into Number Twelve, with its fourteen-foot-high chain-link fencing. Unless an acrobat was involved, there was no easy way to make that climb. No tree limb hung over the fence. The victim couldn't have accidentally fallen in. The compound's main-gate padlock was intact. So was the gate padlock into Pico and Iris's home.

Getting past the preserve's electronic security, figuring a way to insert the body, took planning. *But why would anyone want to do it? What was their reason?* He could think of only one possibility — to threaten his outspoken father. Peter Jepson had many enemies, and Ben knew it.

CONGRESS IV

It had all begun a month ago, when Ben had traveled with his father to Washington, D.C. His father, known as an extremely controversial animal-rights activist, spoke before the House Judiciary Committee about the killing of exotic zoo animals for sport.

Ben had heard him speak on the same subject on TV, radio, and town-hall-type meetings, but this was the first time before Congress.

Ben was proud to be sitting there in the historic old chamber, with its high ceiling and dark-wood walls. The faces of the ten representatives were intently focused on his father.

Dr. Peter Jepson, a tall, rugged man with a strong jaw and blue eyes, began his testimony by saying this: "There are more than a thousand canned-hunt ranches in this country, legal and illegal. The animals, most raised in captivity, are placed in cages or enclosed areas, then killed by so-called hunters for a fat fee. The heads are taken to a taxidermist and mounted for home display."

Ben saw disbelief on the faces of the lawmakers.

"Any one of you can buy tigers, lions, apes, zebras, bears, even rhinos and elephants, just for the fun of killing them. . . ."

Dr. Jepson had let that sink in, and continued. "Where do all these exotic animals come from? Easy to answer. Zoos breed them because their babies attract families, particularly families with young children. The enclosures become overcrowded, and eventually the surplus animals are sold to dealers who conduct auctions. The zoos ask the buyers to sign a document promising that they will never permit the animals to be used in the canned-hunt business. But the documents are worthless and blood-drenched. . . . "

Let 'em have it, Papa, Ben said to himself.

"The famed San Diego Zoo and its sister institution, the Wild Animal Park, have reportedly sold surplus animals to dealers. More than a dozen other well-known zoos have done the same thing, according to the Humane Society, which has a special section devoted to canned hunts."

He then showed video footage of a fifteen-year-old Siberian tiger being shot four times in the sides while penned, then made to bleed slowly to death. The hunter was careful not to damage the head. "The rest of the skinned carcass was sold to a medicine shop in New York's Chinatown, courtesy of the Triads, which I'll cover in a few minutes. Any questions about canned hunting?"

One congresswoman asked about legality.

"The operations are legal in forty states."

"That's shocking."

"It's very profitable. A lot of ranches in cattle-raising states can make more money off exotic animals than beef. They're even raising exotic animals just to hunt them. We need a federal law to put a stop to this. It's absolutely senseless bloodshed.

"Now, for the Triads, and tiger slaughter. You may not have heard of Triads before. They are the most sinister crime society on earth. They make the Mafia look like Boy Scouts. Name any crime in the Orient, from grand theft and merchant shakedown to murder, prostitution, and even sea piracy, and you'll probably find Triads involved. They began in the seventeenth century in mainland China, and they're still operating today. There are gangs of them in New York City, Los Angeles, and San Francisco. My interest in them is this: They have tigers slaughtered for the sole purpose of reducing body parts to medicines, sold under the counter in Chinese health shops. Powder ground from tiger bones is sold to older Chinese males as a sex stimulant. . . . "

Ben had heard his father wage verbal warfare against the Triads and their marketing of tiger parts on other occasions, always ending with, "Help me put an end to the international killing of tigers. Let's save what few are left and put these vile people behind bars."

The committee chairman called a recess, and Dr. Jepson answered questions from the press.

When the recess was over and the representatives began to file back in, a stocky man with snow-white, bushy hair and a deep tan came up to Ben's father. He had a large brown mole over his left eyebrow. "Jepson," he whispered, "you've been asking for trouble a long time. You may get it soon."

Ben was startled. He'd never seen a man's face as strange as this one. Stitched on the man's jacket lapel was this: *W. Billy Caspar, United Sportsmen, Inc.*

Ignoring Caspar, his father said, "Let's head home, Ben."

Ben took another look at Caspar, then followed his dad down the corridor.

Onboard the jet bound westward, his father said, "Pal, wake me up when we get over Orange County."

Dad's always so laid-back and heroic. He could go to sleep during a space launch. Men like Caspar were to be ignored. Or were they?

A few days later, when Larry Templeton paid a house call to the preserve to check on tigress Katrina

Ivanov, who was suffering from leukemia, Ben heard him say, "Peter, you sure poured a lot of gasoline on the canned-hunt fire in Washington. You enraged those people, and if there were any Triads listening . . ."

"They damned well deserved it."

"Peter, call your life insurance rep and add a million."

Ben heard his father laugh. "Just a half million, please."

"I'm serious," Larry said. "You could be a marked man! This place could go up in flames!"

"They know where to find me, Larry."

Now, with a corpse in Number Twelve, maybe they had found his father, whoever "they" were. Canned-hunt people? Triads? Other enemies? But why did they strike last night? Chances were, whoever they were, they had no idea that his father and mother were deep in eastern Madhya Pradesh, India. That was information the press would get and reveal, sooner or later. Would it make a difference at Los Coyotes?

HARRY METCALF

The fog had lifted. Ben left the office to take another look at the main gate and the back vehicle gate. His heart sank when he saw that the padlock on the back gate had been cut and was on the ground.

Close to eight o'clock, Deputy Metcalf pulled his squad car into the preserve parking lot. Metcalf was a twenty-two-year veteran of solving crimes, even homicide. He was stubby and crewcut, with a graying mustache. Like Ben's dad, he was an ex-Marine and wore string ties and loud, off-the-rack sports jackets.

Harry Metcalf had been friendly to the Jepsons ever since they had built Los Coyotes Preserve. He often visited on a social basis, taking an interest in what he called the "beasts." Ben's mother had even photographed him with Goliath, Metcalf's favorite lion.

Ben walked over to the deputy's car. "You hear anything different last night?" Metcalf asked. "Anybody yelling or screaming? People who are about to get chewed on usually make some noise."

"I didn't hear anything up to the time I went to bed. That was about ten o'clock."

Ben led Metcalf along the path to Number Twelve. "Well," Metcalf said, "the jaguars have their faces decorated, don't they?" Dried blood still covered the cats.

Pico and Iris lay on their stomachs, staring out at Ben and the deputy.

"All right, let's see what you think is a corpse."

He followed Ben around to the rear of the compound and saw the half-nude, half-eaten body sprawled on the sand. It was still partially covered by the green drape.

Metcalf blew out a breath and grunted. "My

Lord!" Then he said, "That's something we didn't need. Get those animals out of there while I make some calls. I can't tell if the victim is male or female."

Metcalf hurried up to the office while Ben, Luis, and Rafael entered Number Twelve with eight-foot-long steel-chain leads, a cattle prod, and a fire extinguisher. Pico and Iris would be moved up to Twenty-six, which was empty. The cold extinguisher gas *whooshed* into the big-cat faces and always got their attention. This allowed time to loop the leads around their necks; the cattle prods, shooting minimum voltage, helped subdue any problems.

Soon Ben, Luis, and Rafael coaxed the angry, snarling jags into a heavily barred, wheeled cage. Then they tractor-towed it up the east side of Cat Row. In a few more minutes, Pico and Iris were safely inside Number Twenty-six.

Looking closely at them behind the chain-link, Ben said, "Dad once took me to the Calakmul Biosphere Reserve, in the Yucatán, in search of jaguars. They kill with a bite through the skull or neck. Their leap is called *yaguara*, I remember."

Luis shivered.

Ben said to the maintenance man, "Hose them down." Then, with Luis and Rafael, he returned to Number Twelve.

Dr. Odinga, the resident vet, was already there. "I knew they'd kill somebody someday," he said. For reasons unknown, every time the Kenyan passed near Pico and Iris they'd react violently, snarling, claws extended. Ben wondered if he'd ever taunted them. *Why else would they act that way?*

"I told you those cats were evil," Odinga continued. He'd graduated from the University of Nairobi and from the Royal College of Veterinary Surgeons at Cambridge; he was going to take the California vet exams in a month or so.

"They're not evil, just dangerous." The tone of Odinga's voice bothered Ben.

Lately, Ben and Odinga had been arguing a lot. Odinga had no experience around cats. He had been a cattle doctor in Kenya, but because he could repair minor cuts and treat minor illnesses of the Los Coyotes animals, Ben's father was giving him a job and a free place to stay and study.

Ben shook his head in annoyance. "Who knows

what happened? However that dead person got into Number Twelve, you can't exactly blame the cats."

"The padlock was on their gate yesterday afternoon," Luis said. "I saw it at feeding time."

"It was still there this morning," Ben told him.

"We haven't had a climber in two years," Luis added.

"I doubt we had one last night. Okay, let's start the day. Just stay away from here."

Hearing sirens, Ben said to Odinga, "Please don't get in the way." Ben knew the Kenyan resented taking orders from anyone, but today there wasn't any choice.

"Rafael," Ben said, "go up to the main gate and make sure no one except the cops come in." Ben *was* in charge of Los Coyotes, like it or not — never mind age.

Number Twelve was already being enclosed with crime-scene tape, and a half-dozen deputies gathered around it.

Ben walked over to Metcalf. "What do you think?"

"This early, I can't tell you anything, but it occurred to me that someone carried that body up and tossed it, maybe drugged, maybe dead, for a jaguar snack. I hope the autopsy will let us know. I frankly hope that person was dead before your jags took the first bite."

Ben agreed, but he also asked himself another question. How did someone from the outside know about these two jags' perpetual rage, selecting them for the gruesome meal? Or was it an accidental selection? He couldn't answer the question.

The deputy lit a slim cigar. "How did they get in?"

"They cut the padlock on the back vehicle gate," Ben told him.

"You have an alarm system, don't you?"

"I guess it didn't work."

"Too bad."

Ben agreed. "I'll have it checked today."

As he walked thoughtfully toward the cottage, passing the crime-lab vehicle and an ambulance that had pulled into the parking lot, Ben couldn't believe that the alarm hadn't gone off. If anything touched the top of the perimeter fences, bells clanged throughout the preserve.

Tawny-haired, pig-tailed Whitney Carroll, the

preserve's secretary, was already at her desk in the office, answering calls. Her pretty face was tense. Her answers told Ben the press was already hounding them, as expected. Possible murder? Animal savagery? Did the jaguars eat the victim? *Big, intriguing story. Breaking news.*

He said, "Don't volunteer anything."

Whitney nodded. She'd been through the sniper incident a year ago, and now she was handling the press like an old pro. She was twenty-two and very smart. His mother had selected her. She was set to enter pre-med at University of California, Irvine, in the fall — preparing for either neurosurgery or pediatrics.

"Dig out everything you have on the India trip. Names, places, everything . . ."

Whitney nodded again.

The phone rang.

Whitney answered. "It's your grandmother."

He picked up the receiver, and Grammy Louise "Deedee" Courtney shouted, "Have you called your parents? Where is my daughter?" She was wildly angry.

"Mom faxed me from Calcutta last night and said they were going into the park interior."

"NBC said there was a murder at Los Coyotes Preserve. . . ."

"Deputy Metcalf doesn't know what it is. So far, all we have is a dead body in Number Twelve."

"Your parents must be told to come home. I'm so angry with them, leaving you in charge."

"They didn't know Alfredo would be in the hospital. That's not their fault. I'll try to reach them today."

"Don't excuse them, Ben."

"Deedee, this is all bad luck. I'm doing okay. Really. Believe me, I'm doing fine." *But he knew he wasn't doing fine, because to do fine, you have to know what to do.*

She let out a sigh. A rich Beverly Hills socialite, Ben's grandmother was a former actress and the widow of a movie mogul. Deedee often had battles with Ben's mother. They were too much alike not to fight. Deedee seldom won. But Ben loved them both — most of the time.

In starring roles by the time she was twenty, Louise Courtney had gone through dozens of boyfriends and three husbands by the time she was thirty-five.

"I'll come out to help you," she said.

"Please don't. I'll call you if I need you, believe me. Thank you for calling."

He hung up. All he needed was Deedee getting theatrical and involved with the deputies or the press.

Whitney interrupted his thoughts. "Ben, ABC, New York, is on the other line. They want to send a camera crew in for a program called *True Crime*. They say the people have a right to know about it. The guy says this could be the most exotic murder in years."

"No!" Ben barked, following Metcalf's advice. Then he said to himself, *Okay, okay, calm down.*

When Whitney got off the phone, Ben told her, "Put an emergency call in for my father at the Tollygunge Club in Calcutta and the Kipling Club at Mocha. There's a chance they may not have left. You have the numbers, I think."

"Yep!"

Ben hated to admit it, even to himself, but all of this was so overwhelming that the best thing that could happen to him right now would be the return of his father and mother at LAX. The work they were doing in India would have to wait.

If and when he could reach them, he was certain they'd come home immediately. Just the idea that a possible murder had oc-

curred in the preserve would take priority over the India article, he knew. But reaching them might not be that easy. Their trip to Africa last year was proof of lost contact. They were out of touch for eleven days.

For now, there was nothing to do but try to handle things the best he could. And wait.

Whitney pulled out a folder and set it in front of him. "The name of the Kanha Park supervisor is Gordon Singh. Your mother noted that he retired from the Indian army twelve years ago as a colonel."

Ben said, "Put a call in for him."

THE VI JEPSONS

The fax that Ben had received earlier from Calcutta
was still sitting on Whitney's desk. Ben read it again.

Tollygunge Club
120 DP Sasmal Road
Calcutta, India
700033
001–473–2316

Ben darling, we'll be leaving civilization after an

overnight stay here, a fabulous place from the old days of the Raj, and go to the remote Kanha Plateau, and stay at the Kipling Camp before going into the interior. Your dad and I talked to the Indian press here yesterday and he let loose his usual barrage about the Triads and the tiger-medicine trade, killing of the Bengals by the poachers.

They'd called Ben from New York and London stop-overs to check that everything was okay. They were good about that. Also to make sure their insurance agent had added a half million to the new personal-injury policy. His father had forgotten to confirm it before departing.

"Everything is fine," Ben had said on the phone during their one-day business stop in London. If they were on schedule, they'd already departed Calcutta.

Ben left a message on Susan Trager's answering machine, asking her to have the law firm handle the press, relieving Whitney. He'd already sent the fax from India over to Susan.

Exactly where were his parents? Whitney had their schedule of where they *might* be day after day. *Might be.* Today, unfortunately, they were probably on ele-

phants with the guides somewhere between Shravan
Tal and Bamhni Dadar, hardly accessible to 911. He'd
seen a map of where they intended to go. The only
contact would be radio.

Knowing that Ben could fend for himself, or almost, his parents were often on the go. Most, not all,
of the times, he didn't blame them for being away. In
fact, it was fun having the place to himself. This time
he had almost been glad to see them go.

Adventurer-scientist, best-selling writer, with a
pepper-and-salt beard and high cheekbones, Ben's
father had the lean look of a skier and mountaineer.
A look of self-confidence. He had four university
degrees — *four more than I'll ever want*, thought Ben.

Peter Jepson was the kind of man who said, "Go
everywhere, do everything! Education doesn't begin
or end in a classroom." *He was absolutely right*, Ben
thought. *Practical experience was what counted. Tell that to my
mother, please.* Dorothy Jepson had two degrees herself.

In her early forties, Ben's honey-haired mother was
six feet tall, almost as tall as his father. Together they
made a handsome, middle-aged couple with the ca-
sual, expensive look that smacked of *Vanity Fair*.

Heads turned when they came off a jet. The other passengers always tried to guess who they were. From Hollywood, perhaps?

Ben's mother towered over him. *She'll always tower over me in a lot of ways.* There were times when he wished she really loved him. Maybe she did. She was just too busy shooting pictures. That part he understood, or somewhat.

Ben couldn't bring himself to ask, "Mommy, do you love me?" He was too old to do that now. Way too old.

He was about seven, Ben believed, when she told him he was a "love child," conceived under a bright moon at the Barafu Kopjes, in Kenya, a "king of the beasts" roaring not too far from the cot. N'chi, ya nani, Yangu, Yangu, YANGU! Kikiyu language.

"What did it mean?" he'd asked.

She said the lion was roaring, "Whose land is this? This is my land!"

"Yangu means 'mine,'" she said. "That's the way you have to feel about life, Ben. Conquer it!" She sounded as if that was simple.

Conquer it! At age seven?

But he was a Barafu runt, and later on, comparing himself

with his parents, he was a terrible student. Most of the time, that really didn't bother him at all. What interested him was a life with the big cats and their incredible strength.

Yet there were advantages to being the runt son of Peter and Dorothy Jepson. How many teenagers lived amongst eighty-odd big felines? Heard them bumping against a bedroom wall at night? Lived in a replica of the African savanna? Who else his age ate breakfast to the bellowing of lions and tigers? Who else had a friend like Dmitri?

He loved the choruses as the lions roared, eight or ten times in sequence, standing up or on their bellies; sitting, walking, running. They had a special roaring face, muzzle raised slightly, eyes and ears relaxed, partially open mouth. The sound was always like a symphony to Ben, the brass horns wide open.

Some of his earliest childhood memories were of beige-gold lions, the color of his mother's hair, on the African plains; him sitting spellbound in a Land Rover while his father drove past lazy prides of them and talked about them, observed them; his mother photographing them, going out almost every dawn. He remembered those African red-sky dawns.

Ben's father was always teaching him, with binoculars: "Now, watch, Ben — that lion is grimacing at us. See, his mouth is open, his upper lip is pulled back over the canines. He looks ferocious, but he's only sniffing. He has two holes in the roof of his mouth to help. His sense of smell isn't very good." These lessons weren't in books.

While his mother desperately wanted Ben to go to Yale or Harvard (she'd graduated from snooty Vassar), to "be somebody: a doctor, lawyer, stockbroker," he knew he'd be perfectly content to live out all his years with four-footed furry beasts. There were already too many doctors, too many lawyers, too many computer nerds. By the time he was nine, he knew about big-cat body postures and big-cat language and when the big cat was mellow and when it was dangerous, all this painstakingly taught by his father. He couldn't get enough!

What could college add? He'd be bored and useless and p.o.'d around the clock on any campus. Stuck in a far-off classroom when he knew, hour by hour, what was happening in his canyon home — the sounds, the raw animal smells, the excitement of the compounds, the danger of the compounds. Just what could college add?

Now, there was a loss of human life at Los Coyotes, and what could a college degree do to solve it? Nothing his father had ever taught him could be applied to what had happened in Compound Number Twelve.

LOS COYOTES

Ben took a few minutes in the living room to watch the news. The death at Los Coyotes was on every station. A public-relations officer spoke for the sheriff's department, saying little, and Susan spoke for the preserve, also saying little. Camera crews were already at the main gate, demanding entry. *No!*

Traffic on the county road tripled as sightseers drove out to look down at the jaguar compounds.

KNBC already had stock footage of Pico and Iris, the "killer" jaguars, and it was played over and over.

News of Los Coyotes and its gruesome crime had predictably gone around the world, except to places as wild as the Kanha Plateau.

Coverage of Los Coyotes itself was being pieced together from previous footage, although its actual history was short and simple. When Ben was five, a rich widow in Florida — a big-cat lover — offered to permanently endow a place for Ben's father to study big cats of all kinds in captivity and create an orphanage to rescue mistreated felines, the large variety. Young Ben couldn't wait.

So they traveled all over the southwest United States, looking for land that would look and feel like parts of the Serengeti Plain in Tanzania. They found it in Orange County, California — a movie animal-trainer's ranch — where giant brown boulders looked a lot like the granite and gneiss *kopjes* of East Africa. They named it Los Coyotes.

With the endowment money, they bought 195 acres of canyon country pierced by the lazy little Naranja River and dotted with big blue oaks and dozens of cottonwoods. Had the trees been thorny types or acacias, the acres would have resembled the riverine Serengeti almost exactly.

Los Coyotes was shaped like a fat sweet potato, a long one, on a north-south line in the shallow canyon, with the little river winding through it, dammed at one point to form a small lake for the tigers to enjoy. A guest house with a wraparound veranda was on the shore.

The fattest end of Los Coyotes was the northern extremity, where Pico and Iris had lived. There were various support buildings: a huge walk-in freezer for raw meat; a mechanical shop; a shed for the bulldozer, backhoe, and forklift; an animal hospital; a garage for the truck, the Jeep, and the CAT WAGN, nicknamed for its license plate, to haul the animals, and if needed, the barred, circuslike cage. There was a helicopter landing pad. Close to their cottage was his mother's studio and darkroom.

The compounds were one to four acres each, laid out in two rows. Each held up to six cats. No crowding. The individual compounds were opposite each other at distances of about 300 feet. Between them was an area of vines, bushes, grass, and trees, and some flower beds. The acres were lush and beautiful.

The Rio Naranja was broken into small meandering streams so that each compound was watered by a tiny branch of the mountain runoff. Surrounded on three sides by the compounds, their pleasant old cottage was near his mother's aviary, where she kept tropical birds.

The cottage was on the edge of the tinkling Naranja, and it was big enough to hold their office, too. African big-cat paintings by Kimathi and Indian tiger murals by Prasdan covered the walls. Around the rooms were wooden carvings of animals by Mikandi and Lupali as well as Mogendi stone carvings from Kisii. It was a startling house for first-time visitors. His mother had decorated every square foot of it and had photographed it for several major magazines. She was so talented. Ben often bragged about her.

The living-room furniture — big, wing-backed rattan chairs, a pair of huge sofas covered with soft woven throws from Mbala, and a large coffee table made of *muswili* wood — all looked as if the pieces had come out of Aberdare's famed Treetops Hotel. His parents had brought Seronera, Samburu, Marsabit, Tsavo, and Masai Amboseli, some of the places they'd worked, to the rustic three-bedroom dwelling. Ben thought it was heaven.

———

Murder? Impossible! Could that have really happened here in cat heaven? The idea of big cats eating a human was horrifying. Ben knew that the world would demand to know how such a thing could happen.

VIII
SUSPECTS

Just before noon, Deputy Metcalf finished his work at the crime scene.

"Ben, we've got to talk." Metcalf sat down in the living room, and Ben followed.

"We don't know anything yet," Metcalf told him, "but it's my guess, and the coroner's, that the victim was Asian, female, and already dead before the jaguars ate her. She was probably between twenty and thirty years old."

Why select Los Coyotes as a place to deposit a dead body? Ben was baffled.

"A ladder was used to put her in the jaguar compound. We found footmarks outside of the pen. I also know why your alarm system didn't work. The electricity was yanked at a transformer a mile away. Edison Electric had the power back on by 4:00 a.m., so Number Twelve happened before then."

Ben was speechless. *Why would someone go to that extreme? Cold hatred of his father?*

Metcalf fished into his shirt pocket and pulled out a transparent evidence bag. He held it up. "It's a green lacquered hand. Blood-flecked. It looks like it was carved in the Orient."

The shining hand was about four inches tall, two and a half inches wide, and perfect in detail. The fingernails were painted dark. It was a tiny but stunning work of art.

Metcalf continued. "It was loose in her blouse pocket. Years ago, there was a Sicilian crime syndicate known as *La Mano Sera*, 'The Black Hand.' The Spanish Mafia stole the name, and so did the Serbs and the Chinese. Maybe this little remembrance is from a group called The Green Hand. I wouldn't know the Mandarin translation."

Ben tried to think of the right questions, but none came out. Finally, he asked, "What does it all mean?"

"I have no idea. When you chase bad guys, and bad girls, you get surprises. This one is a classic surprise."

Ben shook his head. *A miniature hand? Chinese? What did it mean?*

"I know what you're thinking, Ben, and I'm thinking the same thing. Someone or some group must be angry big time with your family or the guys who work for you." The deputy tucked the evidence bag with the green hand back into his shirt.

Angry big time? "My dad has enemies that we know, and some we don't. Some people don't like us just because of the cats. The senior citizens in the trailer park next door mostly hate us, but I don't think any of them would go this far."

"Not many people in their twenties could climb a high ladder with a 100-pound body slung over their shoulders," said Metcalf. "The strongest man in the world couldn't easily throw a body over the top of that fence from the ground."

"My dad's been pretty outspoken about zoo-animal treatment this year. A lot of members of the American Zoo Association don't like him. A lot of zookeepers don't like him."

"Why not?"

"They breed exotic animals and then display the babies. Then they sell off older ones to canned-hunt farms and ranches. Even lions and tigers. The zoos make money that way. Dad's always on their case. They sell animals but don't keep track of them."

"I didn't know that about zoos. That's pretty bad."

"Most people don't. It's a well-kept secret. It's a huge business, Dad says. You can buy apes, zebras, even rhinos and elephants, or bears."

Metcalf frowned.

"I don't think the zoo association people would link Dad to a murder," Ben said. "But he's made some of them angry by exposing them."

"That usually happens. I'd need names."

"Owners of the canned-hunt ranches or farms would be more likely to do it, I think. They have an organization called United Sportsmen."

"From what I've heard," Metcalf said, "some of those canned-hunt folks are dangerous."

"Dad was threatened after he testified before Congress last month. A guy named Caspar came up and said Dad was asking for trouble. Odd-looking guy. And then there was a phone call a day later. The voice said Dad was asking for a bullet if he kept on butting into the canned-hunt business. Dad had written a piece for the *New York Times*, calling them killers."

"That's pretty strong stuff. Anyone else?"

"There's the Chinese tiger-medicine trade. It's controlled by the secret Triad societies, and Dad's been on their backs for years. He said the Mafia are Boy Scouts compared with the Triads. They specialize in extortion, drugs, kidnapping, prostitution, robbery, murder, and piracy in Asian waters. They have gang members in New York, Los Angeles, and San Francisco."

"Hmmmm, possible Green Hand people, huh? I've heard of Triads, but I've never heard of a tiger-medicine trade."

"It's a multimillion-dollar business around the world — selling tiger parts made into medicines. Tiger-bone powders, tiger-penis soup, every part of the body. They mostly retail in Chinese herb shops, under the counter."

Metcalf frowned. "What does *Triad* mean?"

"My dad has a book about them written by a Hong Kong police inspector. I'll get it."

Ben returned from the office. He read, "The sacred

emblem of the society is a triangle that represents the three basic powers: Heaven, Earth, and Man. In Hong Kong, it's called the Sam Hop Wui. It began as a social organization in the sixteenth century, but now it is known to be sinister rather than a mystic brotherhood of man."

The book jacket displayed a tough-looking Chinese man in a red robe. He held a sword in his right hand and the Triad emblem in his left hand.

Metcalf closed the book. "I hope your dad knows what he's doing going up against them."

"They've never come after him, as far as I know. At least not until now."

"Don't you have a Chinese guy here?"

"Quan Li. He's a student. Nice guy."

"How do you know?"

"He seems that way."

Metcalf grunted. He shook his head. "*Seems?* Anyone else your dad has attacked?"

"The Safari Club International, a bunch of millionaires who go overseas to kill animals for trophies. The IRS gives them a tax break if they donate the stuffed animals to museums like the Smithsonian. All the money spent for those safaris is written off."

"Isn't that nice?" said Metcalf. "I don't blame your dad for going after them. The IRS is nuts. Anyone else?"

"Well, there's also the Athens Corporation. They own the land directly behind us. They want our acres for developing housing. They're offering big money. My parents told them to forget it."

After a moment of thought, Metcalf said, "Ben, I doubt that either the senior citizens or the Athens people would go about trying to get rid of Los Coyotes *this* way. Any other ideas?"

"About 250 Moon Bear farmers in Sichuan Province on the Chinese mainland. They milk green bile from about seven thousand bears, sticking catheters in their gallbladders. The bile is sold to treat liver and heart disease. These bears are beautiful, gentle creatures who have a golden crest on their chests, like a new moon. Some have been in cages for almost a quarter century. Their teeth are worn to bloody gums from chewing on iron bars to get away. The bears moan and rock their narrow, rusty cages. Dad started an international publicity campaign against the farmers, but they're protected by the Chinese government. Supposedly Triads are part of their marketing."

The Triads again.

Metcalf gave Ben a look of disbelief. "Dad's made the furriers angry, too. He's joined a lot of picket lines in Beverly Hills outside fur shops. He supports everything that protects animal rights."

Ben had punched an El Toro High kid in the face for calling his father a "kook."

"Your dad certainly does have enemies." Metcalf pursed his lips and became silent for a moment. "Frankly, Ben, when any do-gooder decides to shut down multimillion-dollar businesses, legal or illegal, right or wrong, he's asking for trouble, big time."

Larry Templeton had said the same thing. Even his mother, who mostly sided with his father, was worried about the consequences. Everyone was.

Metcalf went on. "What happened last night will become worldwide news by tonight. The writers in that business wait for a juicy, bloody story every day. Death in a jaguar cage is bloody and juicy enough, and wait'll they hear about the crazy hand. That will leak, and some smart reporter might connect it to the Triads."

All true, Ben agreed, with a sinking feeling.

Metcalf added, "Those animals in Number Twelve heard that something was going on at that back fence before that body tumbled down, dead or alive. They were waiting, all right. I just wish they could talk. . . ."

He stopped again, paused, and shook his head in exasperation. "I've got to go. I'll be back tomorrow with some of my people to talk to everyone who has anything to do with this place — everyone. And stop those Sunday tours."

Ben went down to the parking lot with Metcalf.

"Again, Ben, whatever you do, don't let the press interview you. Have some publicity person or the lawyer speak for the preserve. Whatever you do, don't let the press in."

Ben had never had to cope with so many questions. And there was a good chance that sooner or later he'd make some kind of awful mistake. But so long as the cats didn't come under a rifle again, or the handlers who lived at Los Coyotes weren't harmed, he thought — he hoped — he could survive.

THE IX .32

Just before two o'clock, Whitney told Ben she had some bad news. She'd had no luck at all in contacting anyone who knew where the Jepsons were. "I tried the Tollygunge Club in Calcutta first. They said to call the Kipling Club. Your dad and mom had already left there for the Kanha Plateau."

That information confirmed the fax from Ben's mother.

"That head warden, Colonel Singh, wasn't in his office. I left a message."

"Dad talked to people at World Wildlife India and Project Tiger India at least a week ago. Try them. The names and numbers are somewhere in his files."

Whitney nodded. "There's a twelve-and-a-half-hour time difference between here and Calcutta. They're all asleep over there now. I'll come in early tomorrow and try again."

Thinking about Calcutta, Ben suddenly remembered his father talking about making contact with an Indian government undercover agent who lived in Delhi. The man was under heavy guard after breaking up a poaching ring that had reduced Ranthambore's Bengal tiger population by half. The ring had been a supplier to the Triad medicine trade. Government officials had been indicted. Ben would try to follow that complicated lead tomorrow.

Looking a little uncomfortable, Whitney asked, "Ben, are we in danger here?"

"You mean yourself?"

She nodded. Her eyes showed concern.

"I don't think so."

"Are you in danger?"

"I don't think so." But Ben wasn't sure about that.

Walking around the preserve at night now might be a little scary. The "enemies" might be playing revenge games, knowing his father wasn't there.

"Are any of us in danger?"

"You mean Luis, Rafael, Graciela and her kids? Quan Li?"

She nodded again.

"No."

"You know we all saw and heard on C-SPAN what your father said in Washington about the hunters and the tiger-medicine trade."

"I know. You shouldn't be worried about that. My dad isn't worried."

"Odinga said he went too far."

"Odinga doesn't know what he's talking about."

"I love working here, but there always seems to be trouble."

"Only the outside people make trouble. It's not from the animals."

"No, not from the animals." She laughed at herself. "Here I am, six years older than you, and you're the one I'm asking about danger."

"I've lived here a lot longer than you have."

Not entirely convinced, she still nodded.

"Whitney, please open the safe. I want to get my dad's gun out of it." His parents always put their pistols into the safe when they went away. Ben had a loaded shotgun in his room, but it was too unwieldy to carry on the inspection rounds.

"Are you sure?" She was hesitant. "Really sure?"

"I'm sure."

She rotated the numbers, and Ben took out the Colt .32.

Would he use the Colt if he had to? Absolutely. When he was twelve, his dad and mom had taken him to a firing range and hired a top-notch instructor. The man painstakingly took him through all safety aspects of handling the gun. Two months of target shooting had given him high scores. His mother was a good shot. His dad said, "Know what you have in your hand, and hope you never have to use it." That was the environment of Los Coyotes.

THE HANDLERS

In view of what had happened, Ben could only depend on the staff, minus chief handler Alfredo Garcia. Garcia was a forty-year-old born in Durango, Mexico, who'd sneaked across the border at Tecate and first worked as a strawberry picker in Orange County; later, he drove plows and cultivators. He and Graciela lived in a nice mobile home, with their two children, in the middle of the preserve. They spoke softly accented English and were new citizens under the amnesty act. Alfredo was Ben's best adult friend and confidant. They picked guitars together.

Alfredo was still in intensive care from the ruptured appendix and tumor operation, and Ben would sorely miss the counsel of the moon-faced man who was excellent at his job as chief animal handler. Ben didn't need his advice on how to take care of the big cats. He needed Alfredo's adult words and thoughts about the chaos that now threatened the preserve. At the hospital, his face white and pain-streaked, in a hallway just before anesthesia, he'd said, "Depend on Luis. He's a good man."

Right now, on the east side of Cat Row, Luis was clearly shaken. "Ben, someone had to know about those two cats, how mean they are. Maybe someone on one of our tours heard Odinga's stories about the Aztec's jaguar societies. You know, those tales he tells about jaguar-skull altars that need still-beating hearts of victims."

"You might be right," Ben said. "I think the jags were picked on purpose because they're so mysterious. And dangerous. It's the kind of thing people want to hear about."

"The whole world will know about them," Luis said.

"Already does," Ben said unhappily.

Luis Vargas was a hard-muscled little *hombre* with a ready smile and gamecock attitude. He was raised in Albuquerque, and he spoke excellent English, while Rafael Soto, undocumented, saw no reason to learn. Rafael was from Chihuahua, well below the Mexican border. They were a good team, willing to put in long hours with the cats, though relatively inexperienced. Alfredo and Ben had been teaching them. They already had the main ingredient — guts. Days with the big cats were sometimes full of jeopardy. Ben's father continually reminded them all of the danger.

Luis and Rafael were slowly becoming experts at handling. Once a month the cats were rotated throughout the preserve for a change of scenery. They needed to be moved to new quarters with the steel leads, large and small rings on either end; hog handler's canes, cattle prods, and, in case of trouble, the whoosh of the fire extinguishers. Ben loved the excitement, the action of moving day, dust and big-cat defiance. The first time that Luis and Rafael were involved with all the ferocious sounds and open jaws, swiping out with paws, cruel claws extended, they threatened to quit, but Alfredo convinced them that it was all a *macho* game. All they needed were *cojones*.

Mental testicles. Then there were weigh-in days, the cats balking at getting on the big scales.

Sooner or later, Luis and Rafael, with a false step, would be enfolded by a 500-pound lion or tiger, flat on the sand, with their heads locked between big jaws, the foul, meaty odor of big-cat breath flowing around their skulls. It had happened to Ben, happened to his father, happened to Alfredo, and it would happen to them. And either a blast from a fire extinguisher, or the noise of two people running at them with a sheet of plywood or shining, rippling sheet metal would make the big cats release.

Enrique "Ricky" Castillo, part Cherokee, wasn't allowed inside the compound. He was the garden maintenance man, and he'd been crippled by a boyhood accident. As he limped along outside the compounds with his rake or shovel, the animals saw him as a target. Instinct told them that any impaired being was of interest, a possible meal. Any one of them might kill him. Ricky knew that, and he laughed about it. The steel fences were his personal guardians, his bodyguards.

The final staff member was Hudson Odinga, skinny

with a craggy, shining, high-cheekboned face that looked as if it were chopped, not carved, of anthracite. He was a Kikuyu, born on a Dutchman's farm in the white-populated highlands of Kenya, and a goatherd at the age of nine. He was only fourteen when he joined the infamous Mau Mau. Ben's father said Afrikaners knew the Mau Mau as bloody terrorists. Natives said they were noble patriots.

Ben's father also believed that Odinga had done his share of killing white farmers on raiding parties out of the Aberdare forests, so Ben was leery of the mysterious stringbean black man. Ben often felt that Odinga looked down on him as a spoiled brat. Ben should keep his mouth shut, the way African boys did, stay out of adults' business. But that wasn't Ben's way. He was too much like his mother.

"Odinga, you ever kill any of those white farmers over there in Africa?" *An arrogant question from a kid*, Ben knew. *How else did you learn things? You asked. Direct.*

Dr. Odinga didn't answer. Just stared with those dark eyes.

Okay. Ben thought, *you did kill those white farmers. You did! At the age of fourteen.*

There was never a doubt about Odinga's courage. A year ago, he'd attempted to capture the rampaging sniper, Ben at his side. Shots had been fired.

Often wearing a coat and tie, always formal, speaking in Kenya-accented Londonese, Odinga was as dignified as a diplomat. He had crinkly gray hair and a short gray beard. He looked and talked like a stage actor, and he often guided tours. He was ambitious, Ben's father had said. He had his eye on Larry Templeton's job as the preserve's main vet, Ben's father said. *That will never happen*, Ben thought.

But it was a relief to Ben, knowing he could depend on the entire staff during the next few days.

Couldn't he?

JILLY COOMBES

Jilly Coombes drove up to the cottage at about three o'clock. Even though he was a year older, Jilly was Ben's best friend. He wore his flaming hair in a brush cut, and his poster-boy build, bulging pecs, and amazing stamina made him an All-State linebacker. He was also a 3.8 student and was waiting for a scholarship. He had a mouthful of braces and an oval face with pale, tender skin. Ben was lousy at sports; Jilly played everything. They pumped iron together and laughed together and listened to Alfredo translate dirty Mexican jokes. They'd been best friends since Ben was in third grade.

"Why didn't you call me early this morning so I could see the body?" Jilly complained.

"I tried."

"The TV said nobody knows if it was male or female."

"Female, Metcalf said."

"Man, you've had excitement here," Jilly said, grinning widely, his face all lit up.

"Enough to last the rest of my life. Mom sent me a fax last night from Calcutta. I told you they were going over there. I'm trying to get in touch with them."

"So what else is new?" Jilly often came to hang out when Ben's parents left on their trips. He didn't approve.

Whitney's voice called out on the preserve loudspeaker system. "Ben, Frank Coffey is here to see you."

"Oh, crap," Ben said. He and Jilly headed to the parking lot.

"What's he got to do with a *human* death?" Jilly asked.

"Nothing."

Frank Coffey was standing beside his minivan,

which was labeled *Orange County Animal Services*. He was pot-gutted and small-eyed, and he made a point of being unpleasant. His title was inspector, and he inspected as often as he could. He checked the cat compounds at least once a week looking for violations, but he almost never found them. Coffey was dedicated to making life miserable for the Jepsons. Ben's mother called him the Animal Nazi.

"I knew you'd come out," Ben said.

"I'm thinking about getting a court order to have those jaguars destroyed," Coffey said with a tight smile.

"We don't know that the victim was alive when it happened." *Idiot*, Ben thought.

Jilly rolled his eyes at Coffey and went up to wait on the cottage porch.

Coffey said, "You call me just as soon as you do know."

"No, our lawyer will call you."

Coffey was no match for Susan Trager, and he knew it. Ben watched him drive off.

Back at the cottage, Jilly asked, "How did they get by the perimeter fence alarm?"

"Monkeyed with a transformer. They came in the back vehicle gate."

"How did they get through the gate?"

"They used a bolt cutter."

"Can't you get a padlock no one can cut?"

The questions made Ben tired. "I can try, Jilly. I don't know that there's such a thing on earth."

"Have you thought about who *they* might be?"

"Jilly, my head is tired of thinking about who *they* may be. That's all I've been doing since daybreak — thinking. Coming up zero. *They* may be Frank Coffey, or canned-hunt people, or some Chinese guys, or senior citizens, you name it. . . ."

"Look, buddy, if there's anything I can do to help . . ."

Ben sighed. "There are probably fifty things, but I can't sort 'em out yet. One thing is go get us some food." He dug out a ten. "A BLT for me. We've got plenty to drink in the fridge."

"I'm gone," said Jilly.

When Jilly came back with the food, they ate on the cottage porch and then went to the chopping block to help Luis, Rafael, and Ricky get the cats' evening meal ready: "White Bucket Time." The big tigers and lions got fifteen pounds of thawed raw beef or whole chickens and turkeys, laced with vitamins.

About 5:30, after the cats were fed, Jilly went home, and Ben drove Graciela to Saddleback Hospital in his mother's BMW. Luis baby-sat the kids. Alfredo was still in intensive care, so only Graciela could go in and visit him. Ben said, "Tell him I love him. Tell him to get well soon. Don't tell him what happened with the jaguars."

Alfredo was improving slowly, the floor nurse said.

Just after ten o'clock, Ben and Graciela returned to the preserve. Ben began his nightly compound rounds, with the .32 tucked into his waist. The night sky was clear, millions of stars above.

First, he dropped by Number One.

"Dimmy, tell me what to do. When I think about it, I can hardly breathe. The lawyer says, 'Let the sheriffs handle it.' The vet says the same thing, but neither one of them lives here. What's next?"

He added, to the stars, "Mom and Dad, please come home."

Dmitri seemed to be processing the human words and made his customary *ff-fouf* sound, a language of tiger contentment. No other animal made that sound.

Could a human love a big cat? Without question, Ben thought. *Humans loved dogs, cats, horses. Why not tigers? Ben had loved lion Rocky and still mourned his death from the sniper.*

Questioned recently by one Sunday tour visitor as to Dmitri's value, Ben had replied, "Probably a million dollars." But he never thought of any of the big cats in terms of money.

"Aren't you afraid someone might steal him?"

Ben had laughed. "I don't think anyone should try that unless Dmitri is sound asleep, and I wouldn't want to be around when he wakes up."

Almost 80 percent of the time, Dimmy was either sitting or sleeping, dozing under his three blue oak trees. Occasionally he'd get up to stretch and yawn, or play with his golden bowling ball a while. Just after a dawn run was his favorite time to groom, when he'd lick the fur of his paws and back.

On these sweltering days in the canyon, particularly in July, August, and September, Dimmy would stroll into his little lake and submerge his body so that only his nose stuck out above the surface. He seemed at peace despite his chain-link boundaries.

Going up the east side of Cat Row, Ben paused a moment by the new home of Pico and Iris. He shined the twenty-thousand-candlepower light into their cold, unblinking eyes. "Was that woman dead or alive?" Ben asked quietly.

Pico and Iris regarded him as they would a crocodile.

Before going to bed, Ben went to the office and took the Kanha file from Whitney's desk. He'd read it quickly yesterday but wanted to check it again. The park was one of India's largest, 1,945 square kilometers, completely closed from July to October because of the monsoons. The setting for Kipling's Jungle Book, *it was described as an area of forests and lightly wooded grasslands, a perfect tiger habitat. Colonel Gordon Singh was at the Kanha Centre Station midway into the interior.*

Closing the file, Ben said aloud, "Call me, Colonel. Please call me!"

XII

JI LUK

A day later, Metcalf called to say that the jaguars might or might not have killed the victim in Number Twelve. The woman's name was Ji Luk, and she was Chinese. At the time of her death, she was nineteen years old. The vice squad of LAPD knew her. They had arrested her first at the age of sixteen for prostitution. Ben frowned into the phone. *Sixteen? My age. Poor girl.*

According to Metcalf, the medical examiner's preliminary finding was that she'd overdosed on heroin and could have been unconscious rather than dead when her body was lifted over the top of the fence, then dropped to Pico and Iris. Ben hoped she *had* been dead.

"Ben, I know that doesn't tell us who did it. But since the victim was Chinese, those Triad street gangs may have a connection. I still think she was some kind of a death message telling your dad he could be eaten, too, if he didn't shut up and butt out. But I barely know where to start. I don't read or speak Chinese. We don't have anyone in the county department that does. I've talked to a Detective Raymond Po. LAPD has a half-dozen cops who can speak Mandarin. But it's our case, not LAPD's."

"I wish I could be of more help," Ben told him.

"What about your Chinese guy, the student?"

"Quan Li is against the tiger-medicine trade. He's on our side, believe me. He'll help us if he can." Quan Li was a graduate of the University of Taiwan, and now he was writing his dissertation on Siberian tigers for a doctorate in zoology at the University of California, Davis.

"Talk to him, anyway. See how he acts. This one may take a long time to solve, maybe never," said

Metcalf. He added, "Keep me posted." Then he hung up.

Ben had always looked forward to the visits of scientists or graduate students at Los Coyotes. It was interesting to talk to them, maybe learn something from them. He wasn't against education; he just didn't want to waste time in a classroom where he wouldn't learn the hands-on things he needed at Los Coyotes.

Quan Li, who was twenty-nine years old, spoke English as well as Mandarin, French, Italian, and German. *A brain, without doubt,* Ben thought. *And I'm still getting Cs and Ds at El Toro High. I just hope I won't sound too stupid.*

Ben went to his father's file and looked up the information about Quan Li. It was mostly academic, and there were letters from Singapore and Hong Kong recommending him. There was nothing at all suspicious in any of the papers.

A native of Taipei, Quan Li had first come to America as a teenager on a student-exchange program. A friend of Peter Jepson in Thailand had recommended Quan Li to him. So far, he was always friendly and offered to help take care of the big cats.

Like Ben's father, he was an active member of the worldwide *Save the Tigers* organization. No, he was definitely not a Triad.

Ben remembered the second day that Quan Li was at the preserve. He spent it watching Dmitri, sitting on a big plastic bag of redwood chips under the cottonwoods. Quan Li seemed to be entranced by the Siberian, who, in turn, seemed to take notice of Quan Li as Ben passed back and forth on his chores. Finally, in midafternoon, Ben sat down beside Quan Li. "He's the largest, most beautiful tiger on earth," Ben told him.

Quan Li smiled and nodded. "I studied the Siberians at the university in Taipei, then spent a summer at the Sikote-Alin Biosphere at Terney. We Chinese really appreciate the tiger — yet the people of my homeland kill it."

"Yes, they do." Ben agreed with sudden anger. "Or they have the tigers killed."

Quan Li nodded again, eyes steady on Dmitri. "For more than four thousand years, the tiger has been part of our culture. On stage, the warrior Woosung slays the tiger in a display of man's strength and triumph. Today, in Beijing's children's theatre and in Taipei, the tiger begs for life in singsong, and is finally allowed to creep off into the wings. But in ancient China, the tiger was always killed to the cheers of the audience."

Quan Li sounded as if he were giving a professional lecture. He knew his subject.

He continued. "Throughout Asia, from the first primitive cave drawings, the tiger has been a creature of wonder and magic. In the Chinese Zodiac, those born under the sign of the tiger are blessed with the power and courage of the dream cat. I was not fortunate enough to be born under that sign."

Quan Li turned his head away from Dmitri and looked again at Ben. "I am thin and lack courage."

"When will your people stop having the tigers killed for medicine?"

"Some people say when all the old people die off, but I don't think it will stop even then. The mainland Communist government has a breeding farm in Manchuria, claiming it is to replenish the animals poached all over Asia. They lie. Not a single tiger has been released to the wild. They breed, then kill them. There are warehouses of bones from which to make medicines once every free tiger is extinct. It is a forty-million-dollar trade, and it is based on the ancient Asian beliefs that humans can revive weakened organs by consuming every part of the animal. And it's growing, not getting smaller."

"My father gave a talk recently about the Triads. Is the mainland government partners with them?"

Eyes remote, Quan Li replied, "I do not know."

Quan Li was silent for a while, and Ben joined him in the silence. The only sounds were from the dancing leaves of cottonwoods. Soon, the roars of White Bucket Time would fill the air.

Finally, Quan Li said, "In Asian cultures, every part of the tiger — from nose to tail — has its prescribed medical use. Whiskers for toothache; tiger-bone wine to relieve headaches; bone scrapings for rheumatism; nose for epilepsy; eyeballs for cataracts; fat for hemorrhoids; tail for skin disease; penis soup to boost virility. There are at least twenty other uses."

Ben kept his eyes on Dimmy, who was watching ducks land and fly off his little lake. Quan Li's words filled Ben with a sickening feeling, the worst kind of horror.

"Who grinds up the bones into powder?"

"I don't know, Ben," Quan Li said. "It's against the law and all very secretive, even in Asia, so whether it's in Hong Kong or Shanghai or Taipei or San Francisco, it's criminal. But authorities in Asia often look the other way."

"Does tiger-bone powder cure anything?"

"I don't know," Quan Li said. "But there are studies going on, financed by an animal-rights organization in London."

His "I don't know" answers were not satisfying Ben.

"Do you know anyone over there who uses tiger medicine?"

"Yes." Quan Li's eyes seemed to close down. "My father does. I've argued with him, but he refuses to listen. He's elderly, set in his ways."

"He won't stop?"

"No. Like most Chinese, he believes in the curative powers."

There was one more thing that Ben wanted to ask Quan Li. "You know about the Moon Bears? The beautiful bears that live in cages for years, a gaping hole in their stomachs? How green bile is drained from them for medicine ingredients? Thousands of Moon Bears on farms?" Ben clenched his fists.

Quan Li said, "Yes, we all know about the Moon Bears. It is a traditional practice and shameful."

"Why doesn't your government stop it?"

"There is talk about that," Quan Li said, and then he turned away.

THE CALLER

That night, the tiny red light on the office answering machine was blinking when Ben returned from inspecting the compound. Crossing his fingers, Ben hoped it might be his parents or Colonel Singh.

The first message was from someone wanting to reach Dr. Odinga, and Ben jotted down the name of the caller, and the time. The voice sounded Caribbean, calypso-creole. Maybe African? *Was Odinga somehow involved in the death? No, that couldn't be. Or could it?*

The second message made Ben's heart pound. "We hope you are enjoying the worldwide attention being paid to last night's jaguar feast of a poor young immigrant girl in your wild-animal prison. We sincerely advise you to cease and desist your rabble-rousing about tiger medicine, or similar events are certain to follow." It was now clearly urgent to reach his father. He could only guess that the message was from a Triad.

In addition to the "incidents," Los Coyotes had been the idle victim of hoaxes before. But this message didn't sound like a hoax. The voice was cultured, and Ben didn't recognize the accent. He played it back several times and then went down to the living area to awaken Quan Li.

"I want you to listen to something," Ben said.

Quan Li blinked and pulled on a robe, fixed sandals on his feet, and followed Ben back to the office. Ben played the message for Quan Li several times. "Where's that voice from?"

"I don't know where it's from, but I'm pretty sure it is Asian." He looked disturbed.

"Thanks, Quan Li. Good night."

Quan Li nodded and made his way back into the darkness.

———

It was too late to call Metcalf, and no emergency was involved. He'd play the tape for the deputy in the morning.

Ben went out on the porch. The 195 acres, with only the dim tree lights of the mid-preserve living area showing, seemed to have shrunk during the day. Why didn't his parents call? Why?

Ben found it almost impossible to sleep, but exhaustion finally took over sometime after three o'clock. He awakened as usual at dawn, got out of bed, pulled on shorts, and walked down to the living area in his bare feet. He banged on the trailer where Luis and Rafael lived and asked them to take the dig-out inspection this morning. They were up and eating.

"I'm pooped," he admitted to Luis.

Then Ben went back to bed and fell asleep within minutes.

He reawakened a little after 10:00, showered, dressed, and said good morning to Whitney as he was about to pick up the phone to call Metcalf. She looked upset.

"What's wrong?"

"Ben, you were sleeping so deeply I didn't want to wake you. There's a big sign on butcher paper over by the main gate."

"A sign?" He was still punchy.

She nodded. "Painted in big red letters. It says KILLER ANIMALS LIVE HERE."

"What?" *The jaguars, of course.*

"Go take a look."

He started toward the door and turned back. "Any luck with the Kanha park supervisor?"

She shook her head.

"Keep trying," Ben told her, and he continued out, going up the asphalt hill toward the main gate.

The high perimeter fence extended around the entire property. It was on level ground, down a short slope from the county highway.

About 500 feet from the entrance, Ben saw a sign. It was several feet high and plainly visible to cars and trucks passing by. He walked along the shoulder until he was facing the sign. The letters, bloodred and dripping, were painted with a wide amateurish brush. He wanted to scramble down and tear it off, but he thought Deputy Metcalf might want to take a look at it; he might want to have it dusted for fingerprints. It could be connected to Number Twelve. Staring at the sign, Ben felt despair.

———

He walked slowly back to the cottage, rethinking motives, even considering the neighbors at the Golden Years Trailer Park. Some old goat who hated the big-cat roars might have bought a can of paint and a brush. The letters weren't at all professional, just angry and harmful to the preserve. Their only friends over there were Amos and Twist Carpenter. Those two had volunteered last year to help evacuate the cats in cattle cars when the sniper-set brushfire approached. The sign was mean and harmful.

Whitney asked, "What do you think?"

"Somebody from Golden Years."

Ben went into his bedroom to call Metcalf. The deputy told him, "Put on a pair of gloves, go out, and take it down carefully before someone uses a car phone to call the *Times* or the *Register* or the TV people. I'll come by tomorrow and listen to the message. Be sure you don't erase it."

Ben went back to the office to make certain the Asian voice of last night was saved and to ask Whitney again about her call to the Kipling Camp yesterday. He wanted to know exactly what the management had said.

"They left there day before yesterday in two Jeeps with guides," Whitney told him.

No elephants, the old way of hunting tigers. Elephants now carried park tourists.

"They could be miles out on that plain by now," Ben said. "Call Kipling again, and ask them who supplied the guides, and get that phone number."

"Okay."

Frustrated, Ben removed the sign and then went down to search the grassy area behind Number Twelve in case the investigators had missed some evidence. The grass was trampled, and he spent an hour looking around. He found nothing.

A picture of Ji Luk appeared in the next morning's *Los Angeles Times*, along with a story. The caption said she was sixteen when the police photograph had been taken. *She was beautiful*, Ben thought, *with long black hair and large, dark eyes.*

The story, pieced together from a police interview, said she'd been kidnapped from Hong Kong when she was fourteen and flown to San Francisco, accompanied by a Triad gang member, to be part of a high-priced prostitution ring that had been operating on the West Coast for years. Her entire family in Hong Kong had been threatened with death if they reported her kidnapping.

Studying her face in the photo, Ben found it hard to believe that such a lovely, delicate teenager had experienced such horrible things. And just five years later, she'd ended up in Number Twelve with Pico and Iris.

TRIADS ARRESTED

Larry Templeton drove up in his pickup truck in the early afternoon. Larry was nearly fifty, and he was in great shape. The wiry, balding vet was a marathon runner, a fly fisher, and a skeet shooter when he wasn't tending exotic animals. He was all sinew and angles. Ben thought of him as an uncle and respected his judgment.

"I came out to see how you were."

"I'm staying busy."

"Good thing to do, stay busy."

Larry brought out two icy bottles of Alaskan water, the real imported stuff, and they went to the lake house, near Dimmy, to sit out on the veranda in the 90 degree heat.

Ben told him about the threatening phone message, the crazy sign on the fence, and the green hand.

Larry considered all of that for a moment, looking out across the little lake. "The call could have come from the tiger-medicine people. The sign could have been put up by some geezer from the trailer park. You may be right. But the green hand, that's what worries me. I have to agree with the deputy — that body was probably a message to your dad from the Triads."

"But the TV news last night said my parents were in India. So why didn't whoever killed Ji Luk wait until Dad gets back?"

"Whoever they are, they want to disrupt the lives of everyone here. Why wait?"

"But Dad has been after them for years. Why is all this happening now?"

The vet took a long swig of the Alaskan spring water. "I have a pretty good idea."

"The speech before Congress?"

Larry shook his head. "Last fall, your dad alerted

customs in San Francisco that a shipment of tiger medicines would arrive on China Air Lines. He'd been tipped off about how it would be packed and who would receive it. The shipment came in as scheduled, and it was worth two million seven hundred thousand. These Triads, one from Taipei, two from Los Angeles, are being held without bail. The trial is next month."

"Dad was involved in that?"

"'Fraid so."

Quan Li was from Taipei, of course. *Worrisome.*

Later, Ben called Metcalf to tell him about the San Francisco customs' bust and the three Triads who were being held for trial.

"No wonder you've got problems. I'll be over first thing tomorrow morning. I want to listen to that message and check that sign. And Ben?" Metcalf paused. "Be careful."

Ben decided to begin carrying the gun on every night inspection.

Just before 7:00, after Ben had returned from White Bucket Time, Colonel Singh finally returned the calls that Whitney had placed. The colonel said he was at Kisli, a village near the main gate of Kanha, and he apologized for not getting in touch sooner. He sounded very British.

Ben told him what had happened at Los Coyotes and why he needed to reach his parents immediately. "I'm in charge of the preserve, sir," Ben added.

"You sound very young," the colonel remarked.

"I'm sixteen."

A surprised silence followed, and then the colonel continued. "I well understand your need for advice, and I will try to contact them by radio. Sometimes our reception here in the park is not too clear and, of course, they'll have to be guarding our frequency. But I will try my best. Be assured of that."

Ben thanked him profusely and said he'd await any message, day or night.

What else could he do?

DEEDEE
COURTNEY

The next morning a determined voice from Beverly Hills said, "I'm taking you out to dinner tonight."

"Grammy, I really need to stay here. I'm waiting to hear from Dad and Mom."

"You have an answering machine. We need to talk. I'll take you to Chili's."

"I really need to stay here," he repeated.

"I'll send a limo for you. I don't want you driving up here in that dangerous van." The CAT WAGN was a battered 1973 Dodge.

Ben let out a deep sigh. "I'll drive the BMW." That was his mother's car.

"You have a learner's permit. An adult has to ride with you. I'll send a limo."

He sighed again. "What time?" He really shouldn't go, he thought.

"Six."

"Six-thirty," he said. "I won't be through feeding the cats until after six o'clock."

"Be ready at 6:30."

Ben put the phone down, thinking that his crusty grandmother always meant well, even when she tried to boss him around. He knew she loved him very much, and it was true that he needed to get away, even for a few hours.

When the limo arrived at Los Coyotes, Ben sat in the front seat with the young driver and talked about the World Series. "Dodgers all the way," Ben said.

An hour and a half later, they pulled into the oval driveway in front of the sprawling mansion on Roxbury where Deedee lived with a German housekeeper cook and three dogs.

His grandmother came out, dressed in black with a

pearl necklace. She looked elegant, as usual, and Ben now wished that he'd at least put on a tie. They'd make a strange pair. The driver turned and looked surprised when she said, "Take us to the nearest Chili's." Ben hoped the driver would park around the corner.

"Any word from your parents?"

"None."

After they were seated, Deedee looked at him closely. "I think you should come and live with me. It's not safe out there. You've had a murder."

"It's safe," Ben insisted. "There's Luis, Rafael, Ricky, Dr. Odinga, Quan Li. . . ."

"Oh yes, I know. Peter has the United Nations out there, but tell me why all these terrible things are happening? Clearly you're under siege."

"I'm not sure, Grammy." He wasn't about to go into what he'd talked over with Deputy Metcalf and Larry Templeton. The death threat to his father. The Triads, in particular.

"How many weeks have your parents been home so far this year?"

"I haven't counted," Ben said. *Not too many, he'd have to admit.*

"Well, I'm going to have a grand fight with my daughter when they come back this time. I want you to go into private school in the fall, not only because of your horrible grades but to get you away from danger. Murder, my Lord!"

The waiter appeared.

"What should I have, Ben?"

"Fajitas, beef or chicken. You want an appetizer? Ceviche? That's raw fish, cooked in lime juice."

"I know what ceviche is." She looked up at the waiter. "I'll have a Corona and beef fajitas, and they'd better be good."

She waited until Ben ordered, then said, "I'm going to make sure you're going to a private school in the fall. Your choice. Back East, I hope. Andover? Your mother and father can afford it."

"I don't want to leave the cats," Ben said steadfastly. "Besides, I start my senior year of high school in September."

"Let me tell you something, young man. You'll have plenty of time to play with those stinking animals as a hobby once you're an adult and after I'm dead."

"They're my life, Grammy. You know that. Some-

day I'll be in charge of Los Coyotes. That's my destiny," Ben said. *How many times did he have to keep saying
that?*

"Destiny and crapshoots in Las Vegas are about the
same, in my opinion. When I die, I'll leave Dot six or
seven million — and that's over and above what the
government tax people steal from my estate. Some of
that will dribble down to you after she dies. So that's
where your destiny *really* is. In the meantime, the one
thing that your mother and I agree upon, maybe the
only thing, is your education."

Ben felt his usual exasperation. *Education.* That was
the favorite word of the two strong-willed women in
his life.

He was glad when the limo delivered him back to
Los Coyotes. His grandmother meant well, he knew,
but she could be a real pain in the ass.

After the limo drove off, Ben went straight to the
cottage. He picked up the long-barreled twenty-
thousand-candlepower flashlight, tucked his father's
gun into his jeans waistband, and began the night
round of the compounds. Again he stopped first at

Dmitri's home. Ben put the back of his right hand against the triangular fence openings and got an affectionate lick.

Tom Brokaw and others had called Dimmy "Lord of the Kill," though he'd never killed anything more than a hapless bird or two that landed in his space. To be "Lord" of any kill, he'd have to be in the Siberian taiga, Ben believed.

As part of the tour, Odinga would tell visitors, "When it's time to clean Dmitri's space every week, we bait him into that holding pen by putting meat in there. Then we close that gate from out here. He is very dangerous."

Ben scoffed at such talk.

Larry Templeton had written about Dmitri for a zoology journal, pointing out that the world had long been attracted to mammoths, dating back to cave paintings. He pointed out Moby Dick and the Loch Ness Monster and King Kong, and now here was huge General Dmitri Zukov. The world was frightened by his size alone.

The Sunday public tours of Los Coyotes, at $100 per person, were climaxed by White Bucket Time, when the preserve would shake with the feeding roars of big cats. Ben's father took advantage of Hudson's broad British accent. Showmanship! Hudson would say that "Dmitri has the killer's pure instinct, and in the Siberian wild, he would control hundreds of square miles of territory." How did Hudson know? *He didn't*, Ben thought. *But Hudson loved his dramatic role*, Ben knew.

The five-gallon white buckets were filled up with chopped raw, red-muscle meat. Larded with vitamins, the food was placed on the four-by-four plywood "plates." The crowd gathered by Dimmy's compound to witness the attack of the bloody meat and the destruction of the shovel, which Dimmy would clasp in his jaws, either to splinter the handle or throw it out of the fencing. The crowd would applaud. *"Lord of the Kill."* Ben hated the crowds.

Unknowingly, when Dimmy destroyed the shovel used to transfer his food to his plate each late afternoon, he was building the "killer" myth. He was just playing, Ben thought. When he spun the plate away after eating, Dimmy was playing, entertaining himself, Ben was certain. What other fun did he have? His gold-flecked bowling ball? But Ben's father used such things to keep the myth growing and the money coming in, to be shared with the Siberian biosphere for their *Save the Tigers* fund.

Wasn't it enough that Dimmy had to live in solitary confinement? Have no female cat in there with him? Ben had asked his parents about that. Anton Petrovich and Lucy Levitsky lived together nicely, both big tigers; Igor Stravinski with lioness Suzy. There were other examples.

But neither of his parents had wanted to discuss it with Ben. The image of General Dmitri Zukov as a "killer" wouldn't be enhanced by a female who would love him in an animal way. Ben still hoped, sooner or later, to convince his father that Dimmy should have a female companion.

One thing was certain, though. When Los Coyotes resumed the Sunday tours, business would be turn-away. The publicity from the murder would last for years, Ben knew.

THE FOLKS
NEXT DOOR

Amos Carpenter, with his white hair and Colonel Sanders white goatee, got a lot of boos when he defended Los Coyotes. There were shouts of "Sit down, Amos," and "Shut up, Amos," and "It's past your bedtime, Amos!" All of which riled him up. A meeting had been called by the residents as a result of Ji Luk's murder. Seated in the back row, Ben couldn't blame them. He'd decided not to speak because of his age.

Templeton attempted to explain what had happened, but with little success.

"We've had it," said an angry man in a wheelchair. "Ten years of trouble with you people. Now you've had a murder. You need to *go.*"

Templeton kept apologizing. Maybe it wouldn't have made any difference if his father were there, but Ben found himself almost beginning to blame everything on his dad. A lot of this might not have happened if his dad hadn't gone on the warpath in Washington against canned hunts; hadn't gone to India; hadn't reported that shipment of tiger medicine to customs in San Francisco. Who else was to blame?

Then the Golden Years' anger was suddenly directed at Dimmy, seemingly without reason. Dimmy hadn't hurt any of them — or anyone else.

One blue-haired woman yelled, "We want that tiger away from here. We don't live in a jungle. Why should we have a tiger next door? God help us if that killer gets out."

Templeton said, "He's never killed anything. Have you ever seen him?"

"No, and I don't *want* to see him."

There was loud clapping.

A man got up and said, "That tiger wakes me up at

night. And then I can't get back to sleep. Sometimes I think he's gonna give me a heart attack."

There was more loud clapping. Another woman yelled, "You had that murder. . . ."

Ben wanted to yell, "Which one of you painted that sign?" but he knew that would cause even more trouble.

Despite Amos and Larry Templeton, the Golden Years residents began gathering signatures to rid the canyon of the big cats. The new campaign to drive Los Coyotes away gathered momentum.

Walking back to the preserve along the county road, Templeton said, "They can make all the petitions they want. We're legal. But you have to be careful, Ben, not to give them more excuses."

"I was surprised to see how many of them single out and hate Dimmy, sight unseen."

"It's that word *killer*. Combine it with tiger, and you have a powerful description. Some of these people remember what happened to your mother: the scalping."

Three years ago, Dimmy had almost ripped his

mother's scalp off when her new camera made a noise he hadn't heard before. *It was an accident.*

"Ji Luk's murder has started the seniors' animosity all over again," Templeton said.

Ben nodded. "Amos told me this morning that Frank Coffey was over at the Golden Years telling everyone he'd help them kick us out."

Templeton stopped walking and looked over at Ben in the shadows. "I know Coffey's boss. I'll make sure Coffey stops offering his services to the trailer park."

They walked on.

"I have no idea what Coffey has against us."

Templeton said, "It dates back about five years ago when he got a court order against your dad for non-compliance. Overcrowding in one compound."

Ben vaguely remembered some kind of trouble between them. Susan Trager got involved.

"The judge threw the case out, and Coffey took it as a personal insult. He's been trouble ever since."

"That's for sure."

"Be polite to him."

Ben promised he would.

"Oh, yes, and don't worry about that petition," Templeton said as he got into his car. Then he rolled the window down. "Ben, we all think you're doing a great job. I'm sure your dad will say the same." Ben had told Templeton about the radio attempts of the Kanha's supervisor.

Ben went to the cottage for the flashlight before beginning the bedtime rounds. The cats were quiet. Peace lay over the canyon again. There were the usual green eyes as the light swept back and forth. Even the night birds were subdued.

The two vehicle gates had always been padlocked at night but not during the day. Yesterday Ben had told Luis to keep them locked around the clock. It was bothersome to lock and unlock each compound, but Templeton agreed that they should do that as well. That's one thing his father would have done.

At times like tonight, after what he'd heard in the trailer park hall, it felt as if the weight of Los Coyotes' acres was hanging around his neck. Right now, the cat preserve seemed unfriendly and even threatening. Maybe the size of it and all the cats he was managing, more or less, were more than he could handle. He probably wouldn't admit that in daylight. But the darkness brought unease. He felt small and insecure.

Reaching Alfredo's mobile home, he saw that the lights were still on. He knocked on the door, and

Graciela, in a robe, answered it. The TV was on, and Alfredo was in his recliner. "Come in, come in," he said. "Get Ben a Coke, Gracey." Luis had brought him home earlier in the day.

"No, thanks," Ben told him.

"What happened over there?"

"Nothing good. They're signing a petition to close us down."

Alfredo waved a chunky hand. "They have to have something to talk about aside from aches and pains and Medicare."

"What made me sick was how much they hated Dimmy. One woman said she got scared to death whenever he roared. A man got up to say we'd have to get rid of him. Larry argued with all of them, but he didn't get anywhere. Neither did Amos Carpenter."

"Ben, they aren't going to change. It's been this way since the big cats moved in here."

"But why pick on Dimmy?"

"He's got that voice that shakes the cottonwoods."

"I guess," Ben said, letting the subject drop. Poor Dimmy.

Ben wished the Garcias good night and went on to the cottage. He locked the front door tightly, washed his face, and looked at it as he scrubbed his teeth. Same old ugly pan, but there wasn't much joy in it now. The old smiling Ben was gone.

He finally slid between the sheets.

Ben tossed and turned for at least an hour, thinking about the Golden Years people, then about his parents, then about the Triads. Finally he got up, put on shorts, took his key ring out, and went to Number One and entered Dimmy's space. The Siberian took a look at him, then lowered his head back to the sand. Ben crawled into his den house and sprawled out on the straw. It was a dumb thing to do, but he felt completely safe in there. Who but a madman would enter Dmitri's house?

Ben awakened at dawn smelling like a tiger, itching, not sure he wanted to tell anyone what he'd done. Benjamin Franklin Jepson, *el stupido*.

THE CHOPPER

Quiet, perhaps deceptive, seemed to settle over Los Coyotes for the next four nights. Ben had even begun to relax, although all the calls to India had been futile. It was as if his parents had disappeared entirely into the vastness of tiger country. Each day he worried more about their safety.

This night, the twelfth after the "murder," Ben was at Fuddruckers on El Toro Road with Jilly.

Jilly said, "I really don't buy the story that Ji Luk was kidnapped in Hong Kong and brought over here by that Triad street gang. She'd have to have papers to get past Immigration."

"I've read you can get phony papers everywhere," Ben said.

"Why didn't she make a fuss at Immigration, yelling 'I'm being kidnapped!'?"

"The *Times* said her family was threatened in Hong Kong. They'd be killed if she made trouble," Ben said. "She knew that."

"Can you imagine that happening to you when you're fourteen? Taken out of your home for prostitution?"

"Those gangs live by a different code. They make their own rules. They always have, Dad said."

"Ben, it seems to me they would have waited until he got home to do anything like that," Jilly said. "Kill that girl."

"Metcalf is just making a guess it might be the Triads since the girl was Chinese."

They talked for almost an hour. Then Jilly drove to a Wherehouse, where Ben rented Ridley Scott's *Someone to Watch Over Me*.

They returned to the preserve a little after 10:00 and walked Cat Row, moon down, darkness thick. Some cats were asleep, some awake. This night seemed to call for silence. Ben didn't know why. The canyon was still warm.

Back at the cottage, Jilly cued *Someone to Watch Over Me*, and the thriller began to unroll, with Mimi Rogers witnessing a horrible murder, barely escaping with her life. Ben fell asleep not fifteen minutes into the movie, and Jilly went home when it was over.

At about 3:00, Ben awakened to a steady roaring noise outside. Thinking at first that a thunderstorm had hit the preserve, he headed for the compounds to make sure the cats were all right. They hated thunderstorms. Harsh, bright light filled the compounds.

A chopper overhead, its rotor thrashing above the cottonwood tops, used its bank of lights to turn the thick darkness into daylight. Faintly over the rush of wind and the jet motor, Ben could hear the agonized roar of the cats. He looked upward. The helicopter was the bubble type. The rotors formed a swirl in the moist air.

Suddenly the chopper whined off into the night, but the animals had already gone berserk. They were crashing against their compound fences. Some were fighting. None had ever heard a machine like the one overhead; they had never seen such bright lights. Their sleep had been turned into a nightmare.

All the people in the living area had gathered outside. Alfredo's children were hysterical.

The attack had been deliberate. Whoever had done it knew what was going to happen below. The entire animal population was frantic, and the fights between natural enemies could wound or kill. It would be hours before they calmed down. Dmitri's voice was loudest of all.

In his robe on the porch, Alfredo shouted, "Break out the hoses," directing orders to the handlers.

Ben manned a hose with Luis. The cats were out of control, jaws wide open in snarls and roars.

Twenty minutes later, the fighting ended, but it could flare up again at any time. Dr. Odinga would have a lot of repair work to do. A mountain lion with serious injuries faced death.

Ben remembered a winter's severe lightning and thunderstorm a few years back. His father had told everyone to stay away from the compounds, except White Bucket Time, for at least twenty-four hours.

Graciela took the children back inside the mobile home. After they put away the hoses, Luis said to Ben, "Did you see the chopper?"

"I saw it. No numbers. It was the bubble type, like surveyors use. What do I do to fight back?"

Luis said, "You have to let others fight back."

"How can the sheriffs do that when they don't know who they're fighting?"

"We take it day by day and hope your parents call."

It didn't make any sense to phone Metcalf or Templeton at this time of night. The chopper was long gone. This one likely took off without a flight plan and wouldn't have notified the traffic controllers at LAX or Orange County Airport.

Spasmodic roaring lasted the rest of the night. Ben knew that most of the people at Golden Years were probably wide awake, wondering why the helicopter had flown over the preserve, setting the cats off. They probably thought it was a police chopper. Whatever they thought, it was another blow to Los Coyotes.

At first light, the cats were still making noises, and Ben went into the compounds with Hudson to check injuries. They noticed slashes on several dozen cats, but they weren't anything that Odinga couldn't repair. The mountain lion had died.

Outside Number Fourteen, Ben caught a flash of green sticking up in the sand.

It was another carved hand. It must have been tossed out of the chopper last night. It was another Triad message — this time Ben was certain.

Ben knew Larry Templeton exercised early in the morning, so he waited until 7:30 to call him at home and tell him what had happened. He also needed to know if he should mix tranquilizers into the cats' food for the next three or four days. Most people didn't think that animals could be traumatized. Not true, Ben knew. They had nervous systems just like people did.

"Let's get the cats past the next forty-eight hours," Templeton told him. "Come over, and I'll fix some liquid nerve juice for them."

"Some of the cats chewed on one another. Odinga can handle it."

"Have you heard anything from your folks?"

"Not a thing. That park supervisor hasn't made radio contact. I talked to a guy yesterday at the Kipling Camp. He has a small plane, and he'll look for them on the plateau. I hired him with Susan's okay."

"Hang in," said Templeton.

Wasn't he "hanging in" already? Barely.

"I'll try." *A chopper attack?*

He wondered what his father would do at this point. Grammy Deedee was right; Los Coyotes was under siege. But the enemy was faceless, and there was no way to guess what would happen next.

Later, Ben finally reached Deputy Metcalf, who had the day off. Ben found him at his home workshop, making furniture. He told the deputy about the chopper creating a frenzy with the cats, and the green hand.

Metcalf said, "I can't believe this. Using a helicopter just to get the cats stirred up? Wish we could help you with this one, Ben. You have to report it to the federal aviation people. Have Susan do it. And keep that green hand. We didn't get any fingerprints off the first one, and I doubt we'll have luck this time, but it's worth a try."

THE BENGAL

To Ben, the Ji Luk investigation seemed to be going nowhere although Metcalf and several of his men had interviewed everyone at the preserve and anyone outside who might have information.

Life had to go on despite the chopper visit and the cats going bananas; it had to go steadily on without any word from India. The idea that his parents might be in terrible trouble, even dead, was eating away at Ben day and night. He had been hoping something would happen to take his mind off the embattled acres. As if answering a prayer, something did.

On Wednesday morning Luis Vargas came up to Ben outside the leopard compound. He said that Rafael had a friend who worked on an illegal canned-hunt ranch called the Morning Glory, up in Planada, California. The friend told Rafael the ranch had just bought a Bengal from a zoo and thought Los Coyotes might be interested.

"You bet," Ben said. *What zoo? Where? Those were questions his father would want answered. Here was a chance, at last, to see a hunt ranch in action.*

Luis continued, "This is the third Bengal in the last six months, Rafael's friend said. The others were killed, had their heads cut off, and the carcasses shipped to Chinatown in San Francisco." *The Triads again?*

Ben could picture a "brave" hunter taunting the new tiger, climbing up on the top of its cage, firing into its lower back; or maybe the hunter just went around the cage, shooting into the stomach, letting the cat bleed to death. Then he'd make sure he posed for a picture with the dead cat. He'd lie to strangers about having gone to India, saving the head and skin for a taxidermist.

Ben wondered how much money the Morning

Glory received from medical dealers for a skinned tiger carcass.

He was certain his father would be enraged and become involved immediately. *A doomed Bengal. Try to rescue it. Report the owner. Maybe find out which zoo sold it?*

Ben looked up Planada. It was on Route 140, not far from Merced, at the gentle foothills of the Sierra Nevadas in sparsely settled farmland.

Jilly Coombes came over that night, and Ben told him about the Bengal up near Planada at the canned-hunt ranch.

"Let me show you something," Ben said, and he went to the video library in the office. He came back with a documentary that the Humane Society had sent to his father. It was filmed with a hidden camera, jerky from time to time, but it told the story.

The camera roamed down a dirt road along an eight-foot fence, and the narrator said, "Welcome to Rockabye Ranch in the panhandle of Texas, a canned-hunt operation. My tiny camera is hidden in my hat. If I'm discovered, security guards will throw me out, or worse. . . ." *Beat him up, probably. Maybe kill him,* Ben thought.

"The building you see ahead is a hunting lodge where the guests are briefed and shown photos of the animals that they can buy, kill, haul away, and send to a taxidermist. The narration of this film was recorded after I safely left Rockabye. . . .

"The impala, an African antelope, which you will meet, was born at a zoo in this country and was bought by the hunter for two thousand dollars. Her head will be mounted, likely one of several exotic wild game heads in this thrill seeker's den. . . ."

Jilly said, "My God. . . ."

"Wait," Ben said. "Watch!"

Two middle-aged men in their hunter outfits walk out of the rear door of the lodge, accompanied by what appears to be a guide. One hunter has a bow and arrow, the other a rifle.

Talking and laughing, they walk through a wooded area and enter another enclosure that is hidden from the road. A half-dozen impalas are seen grazing. The guide shoos one toward the bow-and-arrow man, but the animal turns away about twenty feet from the hunter. He hits her in the rear with his first arrow, causing her to jump and run toward the fence.

The hunter shoots two more arrows, one into the impala's back, another through her left leg. She hops away, the arrow in her leg dragging on the ground. Two more arrows fly from the hunter's bow and hit her, well away from her head; she falls to earth but struggles up again.

Jilly yells, "Oh, my God!"

She runs to the fence a few feet away and gazes at two black bears in a cage on the other side, as if to plead for help. The hunter drives his sixth arrow into the gut of the profusely bleeding impala. Finally, she falls over.

She thrashes around and tries to get up, but she can't.

The final camera angle on her moist eyes shows bewilderment.

With the first hunter busy removing his arrows from the dead impala, the second hunter, the one with the rifle, is passed through another gate.

The guide and the rifleman stop by a cage where there is a stepladder. They appear to be talking about the imprisoned black bear. Then the hunter mounts the ladder, stands on the overhead bars, and shoots.

"These are some of the people my dad is at war with. They're also probably mixed up with the tiger-medicine trade, selling the carcasses, ready to sell that Bengal," said Ben.

"I don't want to see any more." Jilly looked sick.

Ben hit the stop button. "You want to drive up to

Planada tomorrow and find out if the Morning Glory does have a Bengal? It's what my dad would do if he were here. I know that's what he'd do."

Jilly frowned. "That cameraman said something about how they usually have security guards. What do you plan to do? Rescue the tiger?"

"I wish we could. No, just find out if they've got one and then sic TV and Fish and Game on them. They'll rescue it for sure."

Jilly thought a moment, then said, "Okay, I've got tomorrow off. When we get up there, what exactly are we going to do?"

"We'll go into the lodge or whatever they have, and tell 'em we'd like to know what animals are for sale. We say we'd like to shoot one."

"And the guy says, 'Wait'll you grow up!'"

"I'll say, 'Well, can't we just look around?' and hopefully he'll let us. We'll see the Bengal."

Jilly said, "Or he'll say, 'Get the hell out of here!'"

That was more like it, Ben had to admit.

"Then we'll go find a hill," Ben said, "and take the glasses out for a long look."

Jilly went home.

———

On the big-cat night walk, Ben noticed that the lights were still on at Alfredo's. They always stayed up late. Ben took his beat-up Palmer and went down there. Alfredo had taught him to play the guitar; taught him notes and chords, the difference between skinny strings and fat strings. They were both Willie Nelson aficionados, and the last time they'd played, before Alfredo's operation, they'd done "Take It to the Limit," with Alfredo doing Nelson's part and Ben doing Waylon Jennings's; and "Faded Love," Alfredo taking Ray Price's and Ben doing Willie's.

He and Alfredo hadn't played guitar in three weeks, and Ben badly needed to get his mind off the preserve for an hour. Maybe he'd sleep better tonight after singing some two-chord and three-chord tunes, get lost in the music, singing to an audience of Graciela. He wouldn't tell Alfredo about tomorrow, Planada, and the Bengal. Tonight they started with "Hello Walls," Alfredo picking and singing Willie's part and Ben doing Faron Young's. Ben relaxed.

Later, in bed, Ben thought about Planada. From his dad, he'd heard about canned-hunt farms and ranches for years, but he had never visited one. Tomorrow that would change.

PLANADA

Jilly came by in his old red VW before dawn, and he and Ben headed for Planada, with Willie Nelson on cassette. It was up Route 99 past Bakersfield and Fresno, and Jilly figured it would take six and a half hours to get there, depending on the traffic.

Last night, Ben had told Alfredo, who was recovering rapidly, that he'd be gone for the day. Alfredo had wanted to know where Ben was going. "Just goofing off," Ben had said. He didn't want to worry

Alfredo. Luis Vargas, of course, knew what was going on.

Ben had taken a pair of his father's most powerful binoculars, just in case they couldn't get into the ranch itself.

Jilly couldn't get over the documentary he'd seen last night. "I can't understand the mentality of anybody who does that." The VW bore along in shallow light. "Tell me why the zoos have surplus animals."

"They breed for babies, because baby animals draw big crowds. They're cute, and families come to the zoos to see them. Then the babies grow up, and they aren't cute any more, and the zoo gets crowded, so the older animals are sold to dealers. There are some bad zoos in this country."

Jilly looked over. "They do that? Send the old ones to their deaths?"

"*Often!* It's not unusual at all. People just don't know about it."

They talked about it for a while, driving up the Grapevine and onto 99. *Why didn't the public know about selling the animals? Jilly asked. It was a best-kept secret, Ben answered. Old Willie wouldn't have approved of zoos selling sur-*

plus animals, Ben thought. He was now singing "Slow Moving Outlaw."

The old VW barely chugged up the hills and had trouble making sixty-five on flat land, yet Ben envied Jilly Coombes. At least he had his own car. Ben swore he'd have one next year. He was under orders not to drive the CAT WAGN on the freeways. He cheated now and then.

Jilly said, "I forgot to tell you. Stanford recruited me yesterday. They sent an assistant coach down. They'd looked at some footage from the Marguerite game. I got four sacks that night."

"That's nice," Ben said.

Looking over, Jilly said, "Man, I just don't understand you. You don't give a damn about grades. About going to college. You waste your time in school. Why don't you just quit?"

Ben had barely finished his junior year at El Toro High. He'd just squeaked by.

"I'd like to quit."

"Well, why don't you?"

Ben laughed. "Two reasons. They go by the name of Peter and Dorothy. Mom thinks the world turns around on college degrees. In fact, three reasons. Grammy Deedee."

"Doesn't the world turn on college degrees?"

"For some people."

"You say you think you'll run the preserve some-day."

"Yeah. I will." He was totally convinced he'd be-come the director when his father retired, or sooner. Ben Jepson, grown up, knowing the big cats like no one else knew them. He would be *Director* Benjamin Jepson. No doubt about it.

"And you don't need a degree in zoology?"

"No."

"How about business administration?"

"No."

"How do you plan to get the knowledge to be boss?"

"By doing what I'm doing now, learning by doing, handling the cats."

"Ben, how do you think your old man got this place? He got it with all those degrees. The cats gonna teach you?"

"Yeah."

THE MORNING GLORY

They turned east at Merced and stopped at the last filling station to ask for directions to the Morning Glory Ranch.

"Keep going east on 140, and you'll see a sign off to the left. About eleven miles."

There were fields on both sides of the road and very few houses. It was an ideal area for an illegal hunting ranch, hidden away. Not much traffic. More pickups than cars. Redneck country. Late summer heat rose from the asphalt.

"I know what happened," Ben said. "Some guy with a lot of money put in a phone order for a tiger, and the Morning Glory people found one."

Ben spotted a sign by the highway with a purple morning glory on it. J. AMES, it said. They turned off on the dirt road and went about two miles. Some cars and trucks were parked by a dusty white two-story farmhouse. There was fencing along it on both sides, and a red barn behind it. They saw some horses in a front corral, but no exotic animals. People who didn't know what the Morning Glory was would think they were looking at an ordinary horse ranch.

A guy sitting in a black pickup by the main gate, a newspaper propped on the steering wheel, looked them over carefully, then went back to reading.

"Probably security," Ben said. "He must have thought we were a couple of harmless, lost teenagers."

"Little does he know," muttered Jilly.

When they parked the VW, Ben noticed the NO TRESPASSING *signs all along the front fencing. He had a hunch this was going to turn out all wrong, yet he had to know about that tiger. He had to try to save it, one way or another. It was what his father would do. That was so important now, trying to do what Peter Jepson would do. Ben couldn't wait to tell his dad about Planada. He hoped and prayed he could do that, soon!*

Ben and Jilly walked up to the office door.

Ben said, blowing out an anxious breath, "I'll do the talking."

Jilly said, "I bet you will."

They knocked.

A man's voice yelled, "Come in."

They stepped in. A man in a dirty straw cowboy hat was on the phone. His neck was fat, his head was big, and he looked exactly the way Ben thought he'd look — a San Joaquin Valley redneck. A good ol' boy — probably mean. He eyed them with a frown and kept talking. There were all kinds of exotic animal photos on the wall behind him and big-game hunting rifles in racks on one wall, bows and arrows beside them. Rentals. There was also a small framed note from United Sportsmen. His desk sign said J. AMES.

They heard six faint shots. *Some poor animal just died,* thought Ben.

Ben glanced past Ames's shoulder. He could see the barn, but the wide doors, large enough for a truck or tractor to drive through, were closed. A guy who looked like he might be Rafael's friend came around the corner of the barn pushing a wheelbarrow.

Ben's eyes went to a price list posted on the wall. You could shoot an eland for $1,200 to $2,500; a gnu for $1,500 to $4,000; a nilgai for $1,500; a water buffalo for $3,500; a Grant's zebra for $800 to $2,000; a rhinoceros, $10,000 to $20,000. There were at least forty different species listed. At the bottom was a notice: *Lions, leopards, tigers available at varying prices.*

Probably an old beat-up lion for a thousand dollars. Ben swallowed his anger. He felt sick about the Bengal, and about all the animals there. Jilly looked, too, eyes cold.

Ames put the phone down. "You lost, boys?"

Ben said, "No, sir. We heard about your ranch and came out here to look around. Thought we'd like to shoot us an African animal."

Ames stared at them suspiciously. "Come back when you're old enough to pay me the money."

Ben said, "Well, we could save it up. We don't have a thousand dollars right now."

"No, we don't," echoed Jilly nervously.

Ben was just as nervous, and he knew a lot more about these people than Jilly did.

"Who told you about my ranch?" Ames asked, still suspicious.

"Oh, we heard about it in Fresno."

"That's where you're from?"

"Yessir. Could we go out and walk around and take a look at some of the animals?"

"You sure as hell can't," Ames said.

Ben said, "We just want to look."

He needed to get as far as that faded red barn. That's where Ames would keep a tiger.

Ames said, "Turn right around and see my front door. Get outta here." He added, "An' don't come back!"

Ben said to Jilly, "Okay, let's go." He wasn't un-happy to turn around. Ames's sidewinder eyes were dark and mean.

Once they got outside, Ben said, "Let's drive up 140 and look for a road that comes back into here. Maybe the next farm over?"

Ames was looking out the window at them.

Jilly said, "I wish this car wasn't painted red."

Ben agreed silently. "Let's go," he said.

They found another dirt road paralleling the Morning Glory property about a quarter mile east. There was a machine-picked cotton field next to it, with fragments of the plants and white stuff still on the ground. Ben said to Jilly, "Turn in here, and let's see where we go."

In the distance to the west, they could see J. Ames's faded red barn. Ben said, "We've got to take a look inside there."

Jilly said, with alarm, "He'll see us cross this field. There's nothing to hide us out here, Ben."

Ben got out the binoculars. Jilly was right. There wasn't a bit of cover. They'd have to crawl on their bellies for a quarter mile and then climb the high fence, which was about 200 feet from the barn. Ames would probably catch them.

"Let's drive on up this road," Ben said. "Maybe there's another way to get there." He saw some trees ahead off to the left.

"Ben, I don't like this. I think that fat guy would be more than happy to shoot us for trespassing."

"Let's get up to those trees and hide the car behind them. We can take a look from up there."

Unhappily, Jilly said, "All right."

Ben figured the sun would start going down right after six. It was about two o'clock now. They'd have to wait until it was almost dark to see if the Bengal was in the barn.

Parking the VW, they went through the trees to the high weeds near the Morning Glory fence. "Look at all these animals!" exclaimed Ben. In separate enclosures there were antelope types, some he'd never seen before; several buffalo; longhorn sheep; a rhino; a wild boar; several black bears; and a zebra. Now he wished he hadn't forgotten the camera. He could have shown his father the exact types.

Gunshots echoed faintly from the Morning Glory.

The animals stood there, staring at the humans with curiosity.

It was one thing to hear his father talk about United Sportsmen, Inc., and the Triads. It was quite another to look into the innocent eyes of the animals that were sentenced to death. They'd been hand-reared at zoos, without a doubt, fed at regular times. Most, Ben knew, were tame, unafraid of man, willing targets.

Their eyes were soft and trusting. Ben felt a welling of anger in his throat. Now he fully understood the outrage his father so often expressed.

"This is awful," Jilly said with disgust. "How about the people around here? Don't they know what's going on?"

"I'm sure they do. Maybe they don't see anything wrong with it."

"Ben, let's get out of here. We could be shot."

"We've driven all this way, Jilly. Don't you want to find that tiger so we can stop what's going on?"

"Yeah, but let somebody else do it," he said.

"Tell you what. We'll drive back to Planada and get something to eat, then come back after the sun is down. I'll do it by myself. You stay by the car, and I'll work my way into the barn." *He was sure his father would do it that way — not risk Jilly. Ben needed him to stay by the car and floor it once he did what was necessary.*

"You're crazy, Ben, just plain crazy. You'll get shot. You've seen enough to call that TV station in Fresno right now. Call Fish and Game. Let's go home."

"I can't, Jilly, not until we know whether or not there's a Bengal in that barn."

His father would do that, get in close, see the tiger, get out in a hurry, then call State Fish and Game. His father would stop the execution.

The sight of the helpless animals put Jilly on his side again. Jilly said, "Okay, Ben, you win. Let's go to town, eat something, then come back out here. Maybe we should also buy some fence cutters, snip the barbed wire, and turn them all loose."

"Good idea," Ben said. "I'll check on the barn, and then we'll cut the fences." The animals would be rounded up, of course, but the act would cause J. Ames some trouble.

They found a hardware store and bought the wire cutters.

At a café on the main street, practically the only street, they had a couple of steak sandwiches and talked about Mr. Ames and the Morning Glory. *Why didn't Fish and Game shut him down?*

J. AMES

XXI

Night had settled over the San Joaquin Valley when they left Planada, and some brave talk hid their jitters. Ben was almost ready to back out. So was Jilly. Fools got hurt.

"We need to be out of there in less than an hour," Ben said nervously.

"I'll settle for a half hour," Jilly said, glancing over at Ben, his pinched face showing doubts.

As they passed the Morning Glory ranch house, only one pickup remained, and Ben could see lights on in the office. One upstairs light was on.

When they made the turn off 140 onto the road that paralleled the Morning Glory, Ben told Jilly to kill the headlights. Complete darkness made him feel safer.

Jilly ducked the VW into the little grove of trees that were opposite the animal pens. Two tree limbs hung over the fence. Ben would drop down from one of them, in case the fence had an electronic alarm system like the one at Los Coyotes. Touch a wire, and lights and bells would go off, or at least they were supposed to.

Before Ben got out of the VW, Jilly said, "Don't get any bright ideas and try to get that tiger out. He's not riding home in the backseat."

"I'm not that crazy," Ben answered. The only way to get the Bengal out of Morning Glory would be to tow the cage out, with the tiger inside. "I'll be right back. Stay put."

Ben climbed the tree, wriggled out on the limb, and dropped to the ground. Some antelopes stood looking at him in the shadows but made no move to come closer. They were as docile as lambs.

He quickly went to their gate, opened the latch

from inside, closed it carefully and headed for the barn, heart slamming.

It took him about ten minutes to walk by other pens containing zoo animals for sale. The shadowy sight of them and knowing the butchery they faced got to him again. *He so much wished his father was there with him. His father would do something about them. Get Ames arrested somehow. Destroy him.*

There was total silence as he approached the barn, coming up on the left side of it. No sound came from the ghostly ranch house. The deep quiet rattled him.

There were no windows in the Morning Glory barn, so he went around to the front, hugging close to the side. The wide, wide double doors surprisingly had no padlock. He eased in slowly.

A heavy smell hit him the moment he stepped inside. Ben sensed that one or more animals were looking at him in the thick darkness.

Suddenly, a voice said, "Kid, I thought you might be bad trouble." Lights in the ceiling turned the barn into bright daylight.

Two men were by the door, both holding shotguns. One was J. Ames.

Ben was trembling, speechless, caught in his own trap. The other man was younger, wearing a mackinaw and a black baseball hat. Loose-jawed. Maybe a security guard.

Ben looked around him and saw a half-dozen cages. In the nearest ones were several bears, several leopards, and a Bengal tiger. They were eyeing him.

"Turn around, boy. And put your hands up. You're gonna have a date with a deputy sheriff for trespassin'."

Marching Ben into the house, Ames asked, "Where's your redheaded friend?"

Ben said he didn't know. He hoped Jilly, after a couple of hours, would start that VW and head south — *fast*.

Ben sat in the office. Ames's shotgun was resting on his desk, a wordless message: Don't play games; don't try to run, boy.

The scruffy-looking man in the black baseball cap and mackinaw had left a few minutes earlier. Ben hoped he wouldn't find Jilly. This wasn't Jilly's fault.

The trembling had stopped, but Ben had no idea what was going to happen to him. He hadn't been this frightened since Jo-Jo the lion had held Ben's head in his jaws, threatening to clamp down. *What would his father do? Tough it out!*

Ames said, "Toss your wallet over here."

Though he didn't think he had to do it, Ben complied and dug it out, dropping it on Ames's desk.

The rancher studied Ben's learner permit. "Benjamin Jepson. Jepson! I know that name. Is your old man that loudmouthed troublemaker who has a private zoo down south?"

Ben said, "He isn't a troublemaker. He's a scientist."

Ames laughed. "Not in my book. What were you doing here tonight?"

"Just looking around."

"Come on, boy. I don't buy that story. You were trespassin'. Checkin' me out. The sheriffs'll throw your ass in jail when they get here."

Ben kept silent. Whatever the law would do, he knew he'd catch worse hell from Larry Templeton and Alfredo for being so stupid. Then he'd catch it again from his father.

Ames didn't say anything else, but he put his boots on the desk near the shotgun and picked up a tabloid to read while waiting for a deputy to arrive.

About twenty minutes later, Ben heard the unmistakable putt-putt of Jilly's VW, a noise he was hoping he wouldn't hear.

Jilly came through the door ashen-faced. He glanced over at Ben with a look somewhere between anger and helplessness. The mackinaw man was aiming his shotgun at Jilly's back.

"There are some wire cutters out in his car."

"Oh, ho," said Ames angrily, looking over at Ben. "You were going to cut some fences, let my stock out. Just like that old man of yours."

You got it right, mister, Ben thought.

"Well, weren't you?" Ames yelled, starting to fume. "You know how much money I got tied up in them? Over two hundred thousand."

Ben wanted to shout back and tell him what a dirty S.O.B. he was, making money from shooting animals that couldn't even leave their cages, but he knew that wouldn't be smart. *Be silent!*

Jilly was sitting about ten feet away, and occasionally their eyes met. They both looked guilty. They were guilty without having done anything.

About a half hour later, a young deputy showed up. His name was Jarvis and he didn't look happy. Frowning at Ben and Jilly, he said, "You're juveniles."

Ben said, "Yessir. I'm sixteen, he's seventeen."

The deputy asked Ames, "What did they do?"

"Tresspassin'. They were going to cut my fences. His old man is an animal-rights nutcase."

"Did they do it?"

Ben broke in. "No, sir, we didn't."

"They have a pair of wire cutters," Ames said.

"You want to press charges, Mr. Ames?"

"Yes," he said. "Trespassin', threatening my business."

The deputy looked from Ben to Jilly. "Did you do it?"

"I trespassed. Not Jilly."

"You local?"

"No, sir. We're from Orange County."

"Whatta you doin' up this way?"

"Came up to look at this hunt ranch," Ben replied.

The deputy shook his head in disgust. "Don't you have something better to do down in Orange County? I've got better things to do up here."

Jilly finally spoke, giving Ben a bleak look. "We do now."

"Where are your parents?"

Jilly said, "Mine are home in El Toro."

Ben said, "Mine are in India."

The deputy said, "India," and sighed. Shaking his head again, he said to Ames, "If you want to charge these boys with trespassing, you have to fill out a complaint form. I'll get it for you." His dislike of Ames was clearly evident.

He went out to his car and came back a moment later. Ames rattled on about "no-good kids" as he filled out the complaint.

The deputy was also clearly upset at having his time wasted, but he said politely, "We'll let you know what happens here." Then he directed Ben and Jilly to come with him.

Once outside, he asked, "That VW yours?"

Jilly said it was his, digging out his license.

"Okay. Let's get on the road. Your friend is coming with me. I'm going to stay behind you. I don't want you to drive more than fifty-five. Understand?"

Jilly said, "Yessir."

"I'll signal you when to stop."

The deputy nodded toward his car and said to Ben, "Get in the backseat."

He did.

As they drove away from the Morning Glory

Ranch, the deputy asked Ben, "You have any idea who you were dealing with?"

"No, sir."

"Ames is a convicted felon. He's served time in San Quentin for manslaughter. He's also served time for narcotics. In fact, he hasn't been out for more than three years. He got caught about six years ago manufacturing methamphetamine. . . ."

Ben said, "I didn't know that. We wanted to rescue a tiger Ames has."

"Call Fish and Game."

"I intend to do that, sir."

About ten miles from the Morning Glory Ranch, the deputy hit his red and blue lights. Jilly pulled off to the side of the road and rolled down his window.

The deputy told Ben to get out. "Now, get back to Orange County, and never come up here again."

Ben thanked him and got into the red car. He and Jilly headed straight home without saying much to each other along the way.

There was a note on his pillow from Whitney: *The Kipling Camp pilot that you hired did not spot your parents.*

———

The next morning Ben called a TV station in Fresno to tell them all about the Bengal he saw at the Morning Glory hunt ranch in Merced County. The Bengal was about to be killed, and Ben wanted every decent human being to know about it. He gave his name.

The reporter asked, "Is your father that famous big-cat guy?"

Ben said that he was, not thinking about future problems at Los Coyotes.

Then he called Fish and Game in Sacramento, working his way through the switchboard to let them know about the illegal canned-hunt ranch at Planada and about the Bengal. They'd heard rumors about J. Ames but had never visited him. The Bengal was in immediate danger, Ben said.

The next evening, early, Ben received a call on the office answering machine: "I'll get you! I swear to God I'll get you, boy. I'll destroy your father's animal business the way you've destroyed mine. There was a TV crew here, and Fish and Game this morning. I have to go to court. . . ."

Ben rang Jilly. "Guess who just left a message."

"Julia Roberts?"

"J. Ames."

Ben told Larry Templeton about what had happened at the Morning Glory Ranch and about the call from Ames. Templeton wasn't very happy about the news. "Ben, don't you ever do that again. Those people are ruthless. You were lucky. I'm even scared of them."

The next morning Ben phoned Fish and Game to find out what had happened to the Bengal. The chief warden said that by the time the raid occurred, no tiger was at the Morning Glory.

"You certain you saw one there?" he asked.

"I'm certain. It was caged, in the barn."

"It was probably killed before we got there."

Ben knew the rest of the story well: head hauled to a taxidermist, carcass sold to the Chinese medicine trade. Ames must have connections in San Francisco.

The chief warden said that Ames hadn't kept papers on any of the animals, so tracing the Bengal back to a zoo was impossible. Finding out which taxidermist had the head was also impossible. Fish and Game didn't even have the personnel to check the ones in California, much less throughout all the western states.

But even though Ben hadn't saved the Bengal, the trip to Planada hadn't been a complete mistake — he had managed to shut down one illegal canned-hunt ranch. Ben felt good about that. He couldn't wait to tell his father.

AFTERMATH

"I told Metcalf everything about the hunt ranch."

Jilly asked, "Including the call from Ames?"

"Including the call from Ames."

"What did he say?"

"He said I was a fool."

"Wasn't he right?"

"Yeah, I guess so."

"Ben, what are you trying to prove? That you're as good as your father?"

"Jilly, for God's sakes, I was just thinking about trying to save that Bengal, that's all."

"Your father probably wouldn't have been caught."

"Maybe not. But it was all worth it. *You* saw some of the animals Ames had for sale. Don't you feel good that we shut him down?"

They were in the Jepsons' dining room sharing Italian takeout: tortellini appetizers and *gnocchi al pomodoro*, tiramisu, the kind of dishes his mother would have ordered. Thinking about his parents made him realize again how long the silence had been — and as each day passed, Ben was more and more worried about their safety.

"You're going to tell your parents about Ames when they come back?"

"Yeah, I'm going to tell them about Ames."

"I still can't believe they haven't called to find out how you're doing, what's happening here."

"They're out in the bush. No phone booths there. They'll call as soon as they can. You know, parts of the world still don't have phones. Really!"

"Well, it's none of my business, but I'd think they'd find a way to reach you every few days."

Ben was getting uptight.

"They have no way of knowing Alfredo got sick,

and besides, they trust me to make good decisions."
He said it almost in a shout.

"Going up to Planada was a good decision?"

"Get off it," he flared.

The office phone rang, and Ben got up to answer it.

Metcalf said, "The L.A. police have an informant in Chinatown who said he heard that Ji Luk was killed because she got caught withholding hooker money. She was executed as a lesson to the other girls. And I believe she was also used as a Triad message to your father. I suggest you cool it. I wouldn't even use chopsticks if I were you."

Ben looked over at Jilly and repeated what Metcalf had told him.

"Listen to the man."

They finished the meal, and Jilly went home.

COLONEL SINGH

Whitney's voice was on the preserve loudspeaker. "Ben, Colonel Singh is on the phone. . . ."

Ben came out of Compound Number Four on the run. He'd been in there with Odinga, checking a lump on lioness Chelsea's belly.

He was panting when he reached the office and picked up the phone. "I was down . . . in the preserve. . . ."

The colonel's voice was cool. "Ben, I don't want to alarm you needlessly, but I'm worried about your parents. It's been five days now, and we still haven't made radio contact. Yesterday I sent a ranger team by helicopter into the section where they should be. Not a sight of them or the Jeeps. We'll continue the search tomorrow."

"They had guides," Ben said.

"I know, very experienced ones. I must be quite honest with you. A farmer confirmed that tiger poachers are operating in that area. I'm told that is the reason your parents are in the Kanha."

"Yessir, that is the reason. They're doing a story for *National Geographic*. They can usually take care of themselves. Both of them are good shots."

"I'm glad to know that, and I'm sure that they are capable in the bush. I've read about them. Hopefully, we'll find them tomorrow. I'll phone you the minute we know."

"Thank you, Colonel Singh," Ben said. His throat was dry. He sat as if in a trance.

He became aware that Whitney was staring at him. "What's wrong? Something is."

"Dad and Mom haven't answered the radio calls for five days. Wardens couldn't find them yesterday.

A farmer said there's a poacher gang in the area where they should be. . . ."

After a silence, Whitney said, "Maybe they've moved to an entirely different area?"

"They still have to be in tiger country." Ben frowned widely, the worried edge back in his voice. "Remember Africa last year when they had a running gun battle with the tusk poachers? They barely got out of that."

"But they did get away."

"Yeah, barely. Keep your fingers crossed."

He returned to Number Four where Odinga pronounced, "I think it's a fatty tumor, but let's take her to Templeton for an X ray tomorrow."

Ben told Odinga about the call from India.

"They'll be fine. Try not to worry."

"We hope," Ben said.

A little over an hour later, Reuters was on the phone from London, a writer saying their correspondent in Calcutta had filed a report about Peter and Dorothy Jepson missing in Kanha Park. The Calcutta and Bombay newspapers had front-page stories, he said, wanting to speak to the person in charge at Los Coyotes.

Ben said he was a staff member.

"How long have the Jepsons been missing?"

"Colonel Gordon Singh called us earlier to tell me that there'd been no radio contact with them for the past five days."

"Gordie Singh? He's a good man. What else did he tell you?"

"That a warden team had been sent in to search for them with no results. But he sounded confident they were okay."

"Did he mention that poachers kidnapped a British naturalist two years ago, and a ransom of fifty thousand pounds was paid for his release?"

"No, he didn't." *Why did the writer have to tell him that? Kidnappers? Ransom?* Lying, Ben said, "I'm not too worried. They were out of touch with us for eleven days when they were in Africa last year. They were doing a story on poachers."

"That's interesting," said the writer. "Let me give you our London number. Call me collect if you hear anything. 001-250-1122. Meanwhile, we'll keep after Gordie Singh."

Ben was getting a mental picture of Colonel Gordie Singh. He would be dark-skinned, immaculately groomed, and tall, with white hair and a white mustache. He had piercing brown eyes. Ben wondered if Gordie Singh had ever commanded the fierce Gurka troops.

Two hours later, a *Los Angeles Times* writer called. "Reuters just ran a story that your parents are missing over in India. . . ."

XXIV

PRESS CONFERENCE

The Reuters story about the famous California couple missing on the vast Kanha Plateau was carried around the world the next day, in print, as well as TV newscasts.

At a press conference, Ben said, "They may not be missing. They just haven't responded to radio calls for a week. Their radio may not be working." *This time there was no reason to hide from the press.*

Asked about Indian wardens being unable to find them, as reported by Reuters, Ben said, "It was a preliminary search." *Anything but facing the possible truth.*

Standing beside him on the cottage porch, Grammy Deedee said, "This is another example of the press being premature. The park supervisor is confident they'll be located."

But neither Ben nor his grandmother sounded all that upbeat. Asked if she was worried about her daughter, Deedee said, "I'm always concerned when they go away to the ends of the earth on one of these investigations. I'm a *mother*."

For the next twenty minutes, Ben fielded questions, particularly about the presence of tiger poachers. "I know nothing about them." The guides? "I only know there are two. My father wouldn't have hired them unless they were top professionals."

"Does the disappearance have anything to do with your father's campaign against the Chinese buying tiger parts from the poachers for medicinal purposes?"

"I have no idea."

Both Ben and his grandmother were glad to go back inside the cottage. Both were tense and tired.

Messages of concern had begun to arrive from friends and colleagues everywhere — local, out-of-state, and overseas.

Another week passed, with calls to Gordie Singh daily. Nothing had changed except that the colonel had temporarily called off the ground search. "The Jeep tracks led to a river, and it was obvious that the vehicles were put on a barge of some sort. There were no tracks on the opposite side, and the river is too deep to ford."

"What can be done now?" Ben had asked.

"We have to wait until something else develops, then we'll quickly follow it up. Someone knows what happened; someone will talk."

At this point, the story had almost vanished from the printed press and the TV screens. The longer the Jepsons remained missing, the more other happenings around the world took focus, as expected.

As each day went by and dissolved into the night, his father and mother were constantly on his mind. Hope that they were still alive began to ebb. It was something he wouldn't talk about with Grammy Deedee, but he believed she felt the same way.

He'd begun to think they'd been killed, along with the two guides, by the poachers on orders of the Triads, their bodies easily buried in the earth of the Kanha.

He couldn't put it into those words for Jilly or Alfredo or Whitney or Luis or Larry Templeton. He couldn't put it into those words for Gordie Singh in fear that the colonel would say, "That's a distinct possibility."

Then suddenly it was July 1, the beginning of the monsoon season in Madhya Pradesh and the closing of Kanha to tourists until the early fall. Heavy rains seldom came down in Southern California, never day after day, and Ben's thoughts turned darker. He didn't really know what monsoons were, or what caused them. He asked Colonel Singh.

"It's the seasonal wind of the Indian Ocean and Asia, blowing from the southwest in summer, causing drenching rain, followed by welcome sun. Day after day until the fall, tapering off in September. We Indians have survived monsoons for thousands of years."

"They'll make it more difficult to locate my parents," Ben said.

"I'm afraid so."

DECISIONS

Six uneasy weeks passed, and it was now mid-August, a time when both the Los Coyotes people and animals often felt as if a giant furnace was blasting the acres. Ben was in the air-conditioned cottage with Deedee, Larry Templeton, and Susan Trager.

Though no one had specifically said that Peter and Dorothy Jepson might no longer be alive, Susan had asked for a meeting because there were financial and other decisions that would soon have to be made. A full board of directors eventually would meet, but Susan, meanwhile, wanted to sound out those closest to Ben's parents.

Deedee said, "Ben, at some point we'll have to talk about your future and leaving here; finding someone to temporarily manage the preserve. And, Ben, you'll have to come and live with me."

No way, Ben thought. *Not a chance.*

He knew that the rich Florida woman who had put up the endowment money for Los Coyotes had passed away. He had never seen those papers and had no idea what they said.

Ben said, "I plan to manage it myself," looking steadily at his grandmother. "Alfredo and Odinga will help." His father would have approved, he knew. He had supervised Ben's training for years. Now it was his time to run Los Coyotes.

Stunned, Deedee said, "Oh, Lord, Ben, you're way too young; you don't have the experience. This is a large multimillion-dollar operation. It's way too complicated for you to manage."

He looked at Larry Templeton and Susan Trager. "Larry will help; Susan will help; so will Phil Altman." Altman was the preserve's accountant and financial advisor. *It was truly Ben's time; he was certain of it.* Susan Trager had set up the endowment. She knew what was in the papers, of course. Maybe arrangements for Ben were spelled out if the elder Jepsons were no longer capable of managing Los Coyotes.

Deedee continued, in a firm voice. "An adult needs to be here to deal with the everyday problems, Ben. Your mother told me about the problems with some of your neighbors and how they want to get rid of the cats, about the constant problems with the county Animal Control. About Athens Corporation. And about that crazy sniper running loose around here, then the Chinese woman's death. You can't take care of this on your own."

There were a lot of other problems with animal maintenance that Deedee didn't know anything about, Ben thought. He could deal with them, he was certain.

"Dad had a lot of faith in me. I've been running Los Coyotes for almost two months. I ran this place last year while they were gone. I've been here from the start."

"I know that, Ben. And we all appreciate what you've done. But you're not an adult, and that's who you'll have to deal with. Business decisions, Ben."

"I'll need a lot of help, but I can do it. I really can. I'm not leaving here, Grammy."

Deedee sighed and looked to Larry and Susan. Their faces were blanks.

Ben knew that putting Los Coyotes in his hands sounded ridiculous. But it wasn't. He knew that his father would not want him to leave the preserve. If someone from the "outside," a zookeeper, came in, there'd be conflict. Ben thought he could solve a lot of problems simply by knowing what his father would do. That was how to manage it.

"Look, I know more about this place and the cats than anyone else. Including all of you." Anger crept into his voice. "I do!"

Larry finally spoke. "Ben, I think it's a little too early for any decisions to be made. Why don't we all get together in a week or so to talk about the future of the preserve, and yourself."

"That's a good idea," Susan added. "And in the meantime, I'll look over all the files I have. But Ben, I have to be honest with you. Your father had many enemies. Those people may try to take advantage now. Take advantage of you."

Ben knew all that. He was up to the challenge, he was certain.

"There are quite a few other things you don't know

about. Your father didn't want to burden either you or your mother."

Ben didn't like the direction the conversation was going. He repeated angrily, "Dad wouldn't want a stranger coming in here, even temporarily — someone who doesn't know the cats. I'm sorry, I'm not leaving here no matter what any of you say!"

Larry spoke in a quiet voice. "Let's wait a week or so unless there is a problem that needs to be addressed now."

"There isn't one," Ben said. *None that he knew about. The Triad attacks had stopped — at least he thought so.*

Deedee sighed. "All right, all right, but let's don't leave it too long."

Then she asked Ben if he'd be okay if she went home. In the past few weeks she'd stayed at Los Coyotes often, going back to Beverly Hills each day to take care of her three dogs.

"I'll be fine," he said. *Fine but lonely, except for the cats.*

"Can you feed yourself?"

He laughed. "Yes, Grandmother. Don't be ridiculous."

Templeton asked, "Do you need any money?"

"A little. I'm starting to run short." He hadn't been

thinking about money. Since his parents left, he'd been using the compound petty cash, but that was nearly gone. The staff had been paid because Whitney took care of the salaries. She drew all the checks.

Susan said, "I'll take care of that tomorrow. Have Whitney call me."

Maybe things would settle down now. He hoped they would.

Right now, Ben needed to get back to work with Luis, Rafael, and Ricky. It was nearing White Bucket Time, and already the cats were moving around restlessly, muttering and occasionally roaring. They knew the hour was near.

Jilly came over about 7:30 to pump iron with Ben.

He said to Jilly, "I've got a very bad thing on my mind, and I think it'll be with me as long as I live. Remember how many times Whitney and I tried to contact my dad and mom over there, the calls, the air search for them?"

"Yes."

"I was worried sick about them, and one night I thought that if anything had happened to them, let it be to my mother."

"Ben, don't do this to yourself."

"I can't help it. That was kind of a death wish."

"It wasn't any death wish, Ben. Don't do this to yourself. Please don't."

"You don't understand."

"Yes, I do. The very last thing your parents would want you to do is blame yourself."

He shook his head and said, barely audible, "You don't understand."

But he knew Jilly did understand.

That night, he imagined his parents huddling in the jungle, wind swaying the trees, rain pouring over them. Ben called out, and his father raised his head to call back. Then the dream ended.

THE MEETING

Another week went by, and the meeting to determine the immediate future of Los Coyotes Preserve was called for five o'clock.

"I'm a little scared," Ben told Luis. "They're going to talk about a temporary boss."

Luis said gravely, "I hope it is you."

"So do I," Ben said, taking a deep breath. He knew the odds were against him because of his age. More than anything else, he wanted to keep staying at Los Coyotes; live where he was living in the cottage, do what he was doing until his parents came back. *He knew they'd come back. They had to.* In the end, that's all he'd ask — to stay where he was, indefinitely. Not give up the house and cats to some stranger.

Deedee, Susan, banker Steve Manahan, accountant Phil Altman, and meat supplier Al Levine were already gathered when Ben came through the front door. They all greeted him affectionately. Larry Templeton had phoned he'd be along.

They were the board of directors, and they met four times a year. He had never been invited to attend but had usually heard bits and pieces of what went on.

"And how are the cats, Ben?" Susan asked.

"Fine. Trudy has a bad cold, and Sasha Kurskaya has a carbuncle."

There was laughter.

Also in the living room were Alfredo Garcia and Hudson Odinga. Ben was a little surprised to see them sitting there. *Who'd asked them? Susan?*

In this room, where his father and mother were still so present — their paintings, wooden statues, exotic furniture — Ben tried to hold back tears. He could feel his parents in a strange way, living, not dead. But there.

He looked over at Deedee. She was swallowing hard.

Susan Trager began the meeting. "Mrs. Gaines, who put up the five-million-dollar grant for the preserve, specified that at least two million of it be invested in safe securities, the other three million to be used for land purchase and creation of the home for orphaned big cats. Your father, Ben, became director until such time as he chose not to be, or became incapacitated or was deceased. The board of directors would then choose a qualified successor. I have a copy of that document for you, Ben. The others have theirs already."

She passed one to Ben. She was all business.

Ben swallowed and felt a punch in the gut coming, words that he did not want to hear. He wanted to walk out, flee. "Does that paper say the director has to have a degree?"

"Mrs. Gaines did not specify a college degree. Ben, if you were twenty-one and had a college degree, we'd vote here today on whether or not you could temporarily assume your father's job. But because you're a minor, for legal purposes alone, you're not allowed to run the preserve beyond what you're already doing. The other board members agree."

She must have polled them by phone, he thought. Ben felt helpless. "But why not let it be run without a director for now? You be acting director. I'll just do all the physical stuff. See that the cats are taken care of. Do everything that my dad did except for the business stuff."

"I'm afraid that won't work either. I have no experience in running this place. But it will take time to find a temporary qualified person who can, so in the meantime, we'd all appreciate your help in keeping things under control until we do. You, Alfredo, and Dr. Odinga . . ."

Ben interrupted. "I'm not going to be kicked out of this house, am I?" The cottage was part of the preserve.

"Of course not, or at least not until we find an interim director," Susan replied.

Ben felt demolished.

Susan said the board was going into "executive session," and that they needed Ben, Alfredo, and Odinga to leave the room.

Outside, Alfredo gave Ben a hug. "I'm sorry about all this. What do you think they're talking about now?"

Odinga said, "Has something to do with us."

Ben remained silent. Los Coyotes was slipping away from him. All his parents had worked for was slipping away, too. Maybe he could buy a trailer and put it alongside Alfredo's? The new director probably wouldn't want the son of the founder on the property. He walked away from Alfredo and Odinga to sit by himself on a bench. He felt despondent and defeated.

After almost half an hour, Susan called them back inside to announce that Ben's salary would increase from $400 a week to total $500; Odinga's would increase to $400, and Alfredo's an additional $250, bringing the chief handler rightfully up to $750 a week.

The meeting ended with Susan saying she'd immediately be seeking a candidate for the interim job. She said she was certain that the preserve had a bright future. Then she walked over to Ben and put an arm around his shoulder. "I'll make certain you can live on the premises as long as you want to."

She talks as if my parents are dead, Ben thought. *As if*

they're never coming back. And what she didn't say during the meeting was that perhaps the troubles at Los Coyotes are in the past because my dad is still missing.

Jilly called later that afternoon. "You the big boss now?"

"I can take Ricky's place and scoop up cat poop, or I can be chief cat feeder," Ben said with disgust.

"You didn't get it?"

"By five years and a college degree."

"Don't take it too hard."

"I already have." Then he added, "I think I'll drop out of school. I need to be around the preserve all the time now." His senior year would begin in less than a month.

"Don't you dare, Ben! Your mom and dad would be sick."

"They aren't here," Ben said angrily.

"Don't use what's happened as an excuse."

"School is a waste of time for me," Ben said. "Always has been."

"It isn't. Not at all. Your parents want you to go to college. I'm sure you'll have college money."

"I'll give it to someone who needs it."

"If you have a college degree when you're twenty-one, you can take over."

"Fat chance," Ben said. "Whoever comes in will have a lock on it by that time, whether I go to college or not."

"You're not making sense, Ben."

"I am for me."

Jilly groaned.

"My parents can't live my life for me, especially now."

"No, they can't.

Ben sat in silence for a moment, then said, "You know what, Jilly? To finish this day off, I'd like to take Dimmy out for a long walk tonight, let him be free for the first time in six years."

"Walk Dimmy? Ben, are you all right?"

Ben laughed softly, in futility.

Gordie Singh called the next morning and took a moment just to chat. How was Ben doing? How was the weather? How were the cats? Then Colonel Singh said, "I don't want you to get your hopes up, but I got a report yesterday that a surplus military truck, an old one, had two Caucasians as passengers, a male and a female, along with four men described as natives. The truck was on Highway 26 near Mukki. I'm investigating because Caucasian tourists don't usually ride in our old trucks with locals. . . ."

Ben's voice shook with anxiety. "Please find out about them."

"I promise," Singh said.

Ben thought about the call all day. Maybe there was hope, after all? Maybe they were alive?

A SIGHTSEER?

Ben went out to shop for frozen dinners, and when he returned, a black Ford Explorer was parked up on the lonely county road above Los Coyotes. The memories of Ji Luk and the chopper were still very fresh, and Ben went on past the high chain-link gate for about a mile, then turned around and headed back for a better look at the SUV. His father had always worried about any vehicles parked above the big-cat compounds, especially at night. In the daylight hours, tourists often stopped to look down the steep banks in hopes of seeing animals. Maybe the troubles at Los Coyotes weren't over.

Ben slowed up, approaching the car. It had a California plate encased in a San Francisco holder. No one seemed to be in or around the Explorer, and that made him uneasy.

Ben drove on home. The only lights shone from the cottage and the front gate, with three more illuminating the short downhill driveway. Beyond that, the preserve was like the inside of a coal mine when the moon was down.

He went into the cottage, pulled the Colt out from under his bed, got the high-power flashlight from its place by the front door, and went out for the usual nighttime inspection. He glanced up at the road several times, but the black car blended into the darkness. He thought again of the young Chinese woman and the chopper. Was that all in the past now, or would there someday be an explanation?

He saw movement in the parking lot, causing his heart to drum. He aimed the Colt and switched on the flashlight, catching a startled Quan Li in the intense beam. Li's mouth was wide open in surprise, and his hands were in a guilty stick-em-up mode. His face was chalk white.

"What are you doing out here?" Ben asked.

"Taking a walk to get away from my studies," Quan Li said. "I do it now and then. It is peaceful and quiet."

"It may also be dangerous right now."

He noticed that Li was looking at the Colt, and he lowered it.

"I hadn't thought about that."

"All of us are still jumpy," Ben told him.

Li nodded. "I would think so."

"There's a black Explorer parked up on the road," Ben said. "It has San Francisco license plates. Anyone you know, Li?"

Li didn't react. His dark eyes registered zero. "No."

Ben switched off the light. "Good night, Quan Li. I'm sorry if I scared you."

"G'night." Quan Li swiftly walked away into the darkness.

Ben walked on toward Dmitri's enclosure. *There was no reason for Quan Li not to take some fresh air at night. Or was there?*

The tiger's eyes glistened. Little of him could be seen in the black thickness. *Wanna come in and sleep with me?*

Ben looked back up the embankment, toward the parked Explorer, and shook his head. After he'd said good night to General Dmitri Zukov, Ben continued the inspection and returned to the cottage, locking the door.

He'd ask Jilly Coombes to come and stay for a week. They could pump some more iron, have a few laughs. With Jilly there he'd feel safer.

Ben stayed awake a long time, listening for any noise that wasn't ordinary, again thinking about his mother and father. Maybe he'd do that for the rest of his life.

Finally, he fell asleep.

He awakened screaming a few hours later. He was in Number Twelve with Pico and Iris and Ji Luk. She was still alive.

The nightmare left him in a cold sweat.

XXVIII

DR. PAUL GROVER

Susan Trager brought the first candidate for interim director to Los Coyotes and asked Ben to show him around. *He'd show him around all right, answer his questions, but volunteer nothing.*

Dr. Paul Grover was the assistant director of the San Antonio Zoo. He was in his forties, graying, and overweight. Wearing a brown suit, he didn't look like a big-cat man. Ben disliked him from the moment Susan led him through the cottage door. Ben didn't think he'd like anyone she brought in.

"Ben, I'm so sorry about your parents. I hope they'll

be found. I met your father once long ago, and I admire him greatly. I've read his books."

Ben thanked him for his kind words, but he had heard that the San Antonio Zoo had openly sold exotic animals to hunt farms. Not much of a recommendation, in Ben's opinion. He'd tell Susan about it when he had a chance. He'd sabotage Dr. Paul Grover.

At Number One, Ben said, "This is Dmitri."

"Oh, yes, I've heard of him. He's spectacular."

"More than that," Ben said. "Would you like to go in with him?"

Grover laughed. "Not this trip."

Or any other trip, Ben thought.

They wound in and out of the preserve, Ben tight-lipped. He delivered the zoologist back to the cottage after less than an hour.

It had been a rotten week. Why couldn't everyone understand that he and Alfredo and Odinga could handle Los Coyotes, aside from finances? It wasn't necessary to bring in prissy "doctors" like Grover. Hadn't Ben been tested long ago, beginning with the sniper? Hadn't he been tested lately?

He called Susan after she returned to her office, and

he told her about Grover and the canned-hunt con-nections.

She was alarmed. "I had no idea, Ben, that his zoo sold off exotic animals. Obviously he's not at all what we're looking for."

"He isn't. He's not a big-cat man. I wish you'd leave things the way they are."

"Ben, the board has decided that the interim posi-tion has to be filled by a university-trained zoologist. It's a place for scientific study. You know that."

"We only had two graduate students last year. Quan Li is here now. There's just one more scheduled for late fall, a German."

"Ben, it's a matter of prestige. Try to understand. If we could do it, I'd vote for Alfredo today."

He believed her. *Why, oh why, did his parents have to go to India?*

DMITRI IS OUT

Hearing a voice outside shout, "Ben! Ben!" Ben fought his way out of sleep. He was groggy, and his mouth was parched.

He rolled off the bed and staggered naked to the front door. "Okay, okay . . ." he said impatiently to the voice on the porch.

Opening the door, he saw Luis. His brown skin had whitened with fear.

"Dmitri is out. . . ."

Dmitri is out! Ben wondered if he was still in bed,

having another terrible nightmare. He couldn't speak for a few seconds. *Was Luis insane?*

Luis repeated, "Ben, Dimmy is out, for God's sake."

"He can't be. He was locked in last night. I checked every lock."

"Ben, he's *out!* Do you hear me?"

"Stay here."

Ben ran back to his bedroom, pulled on pants and Uggs, and ran, shirtless, back to the porch. Then he went back inside for the pistol, thinking the unthinkable. Shoot Dimmy if he attacked anyone? The Colt was useless. Bad idea. Only a big-game rifle would stop him.

"Alfredo and Ricky are already looking for him," Luis said.

Pray to God he was still inside the preserve fences. Dmitri had been in captivity for more than six years. Free, he just might be curious. Everything would be new to him. Every smell, every tree. His only contact with humans had been Ben's father and mother, and Ben himself. Who knew what would happen if he got outside?

They reached Compound Number One. The gate was wide open. The padlock was blackened, torch cut. Someone had let him loose on purpose. *The Triads?*

It could not have happened! But it had happened on purpose. And maybe Dimmy was a killer after all.

Alfredo and Ricky ran up. Alfredo's face was filled with fear. "Ben, what do we do?"

"We search every single foot of land, go into every open building. Have you made sure both gates are closed and locked?"

"Ben, the front gate was open. The lock was cut through with a torch. I closed it. The back one was closed and locked."

"My God, Alfredo, he may be outside the preserve."

Alfredo nodded.

Ben thought a moment. "All of you get inside Alfredo's place. I know Dimmy, Dimmy knows me. I don't think he'll hurt me. Give me your lead, Luis."

Alfredo said, "Ben, I have to go with you."

"No, you're still recovering from your surgery. Dmitri could break your neck with one swat, literally cut off your head with one bite. Go! Rafael, Luis, Ricky, now! Tell Odinga and Quan Li to stay inside, too."

Ben started to wind through the compounds, softly calling out, "Dimmy, Dimmy . . ."

He'd make a thorough search of all the compound areas and buildings, then complete it by circling the outer fence. But he hadn't gone fifty feet when he thought of Whitney. She'd be coming to work about nine o'clock, having no idea that Dmitri was loose; then Jilly would come an hour later.

He ran back to the office, got a new padlock, scribbled a note, *Quarantined*, and ran to the main gate. Whitney would know something had happened; Jilly would know, too. It was too soon to call Larry and Metcalf.

Resuming the search, he tried to slow down his thinking. He imagined putting a chain around the Siberian's neck and saying, calmly, "Come with me, Dimmy." It might work with only one person on earth. Himself.

As he walked, trying to breathe normally, with every nerve tingling, he kept calling out to Dmitri.

It took almost an hour and a half to complete the compound and building search; to walk around nearly a mile of exterior fencing. Dimmy had vanished, and Ben now faced the worst fear of all. The tiger must have gotten outside the preserve.

If Dmitri had gone east, that new Athens upscale housing development was within four miles, with a golf course. Humans. A lot of humans. Women, children, dogs, cats!

Ben felt an icy chill. He pictured an 800-pound tiger moving along the million-dollar homes of Coto de Viejo: baby-boomer, yuppie land. The picture was unthinkable.

What was more likely was this: Dimmy attacking some hapless human and being shot by law enforcement officers. For everyone's sake, Ben hoped for the latter. Organizing a hunt for the Siberian was not an option.

Ben ended the search back at Number One. He examined the padlock. The smell of the torch was still on the metal. *Who had done this in a final attempt to close down Los Coyotes? The Triads? United Sportsmen and W. Billy Caspar? J. Ames? An obsessed Frank Coffey? Whoever it was had to know that the courts would order an end to keeping the big cats if they were endangering countless lives.*

But how did *they* get in? A sophisticated new system had been installed and tested repeatedly. It had a battery backup in case regular power was shut off. This likely meant that someone inside the preserve knew how the system operated and shut it down. Ben couldn't believe that any of the handlers were involved. That left Odinga or Quan Li. But the immediate crisis was Dmitri. *Where was he?*

Ben stood still a minute. For the first time, he saw the tire tracks in the dew-damp sand that backed up to the compound. He followed them up the little hill to the main gate. *Dmitri had been kidnapped! It was hard to believe, but there was no other answer. Incredible, impossible, unbelievable: the world's largest, most valuable tiger, Lord of the Kill, stolen?*

He must have been tranquilized, hauled out of Number One on a special gurney, transferred to a truck that held a cage, and hauled away. Simply to get him on the gurney would have taken at least four or five strong men. Had J. Ames organized it? The Triads?

Ben was breathless at the thought. *The Lord of the Kill stolen like a huge, breathing diamond.*

He raced to Alfredo's, and told all of them, Graciela, the children, Alfredo, Odinga, Luis, Rafael and Ricky, that Dimmy had been stolen. They looked at him with disbelief. He didn't blame them. Cars were stolen, Brink's armored vans were stolen, airplanes were stolen, but not Siberian tigers; not one this size.

He ran to the office. There was a message from Whitney. She and Jilly were both at a coffee shop on eastern El Toro Road. He called Whitney and told her that Dimmy had been kidnapped.

"Are you kidding me?" She was incredulous.

"I wish I were."

Then he placed a call to Metcalf, but the deputy was out. "Please get in touch with him and ask him to call me. It's an emergency. Please track him down."

DEPUTY METCALF AGAIN

Metcalf couldn't believe it when Ben told him about Dmitri. "That's like somebody stealing a whale, Ben. That's like stealing King Kong."

Ben raised his voice. "He's gone, and he didn't get out by himself, believe me. It happened sometime last night."

"Ben, I've seen Dmitri a dozen times. He weighs about 800 pounds, doesn't he?"

"Yes, Mr. Metcalf, he does. Somebody would have to tranquilize him and take him out of the compound in a zoo cage, which would have to be on wheels inside a truck."

There was a silence while the deputy considered what Ben had just said. "Any idea why anyone in his right mind would steal an 800-pound killer tiger?"

Ben frowned and hesitated. "Maybe the Triads? Just why they'd do it, I don't know. Maybe for the money? Maybe just to hassle us some more. . . ."

"Ben, are you absolutely, absolutely certain that the tiger didn't get out by mistake — that someone didn't do something stupid and leave his gate open? If we've got Dmitri running around loose . . ."

"I can show you where someone took a torch to the padlock. I can show you the tire tracks, dual wheels of a truck."

"And all of you slept through it? You didn't hear anything? No voices? No engine sounds?"

"The cottage is about a hundred yards from Number One, and Alfredo's place is about the same. Whoever did it knew what they were doing. Everyone *did* sleep through it."

Metcalf sighed. "I'll take your word. How much do you think Dmitri is worth?"

"My father had an offer on him from Ringling Brothers at five hundred thousand dollars. There was a Las Vegas hotel casino that offered twenty thousand a month for lobby display. He's probably worth at least a million to Chinese medical dealers. They could advertise that he was the strongest tiger in the world. His body parts would be a gold mine in Singapore, Hong Kong, or Taipei."

"Have there been any messages this morning asking for ransom money?"

"No, sir."

"I still can't believe it, but it sounds like he was kidnapped," Metcalf said. "We've got more crazies in this fool state than are in all the looney bins around the world."

"It *has* to be kidnapping," Ben said.

"You know the press will have another field day with this, an animal that big and dangerous swiped from a big-cat park. They'll think it's a publicity stunt. First question is why the new alarm system blew it."

"It must have taken an expert to short-circuit it this time. Is it possible that someone with the security company was being paid off?"

"Maybe. That's happened before. We'll worry about that later. Our first concern is finding out where that stolen cat is now, right now. I'll come out as soon as I can."

Jilly and Whitney pulled in right after Ben hung up. They both still couldn't believe that Dmitri wasn't down in Number One. "Stealing a big tiger seems impossible. Where do you put it after you steal it?" Jilly said.

"I have no idea."

Metcalf arrived within an hour, followed by a sheriff's photographer.

Ben took him to vacated Number One and up to the main gate. Metcalf shook his head. "Guys that I work with are already making tiger-napping jokes. No one believes it. How many men would it take to lift him up?"

"Four or five could roll him, if he was tranquilized. Whoever swiped Dmitri had to be experienced in handling big cats. I'm certain of that. Just putting him to sleep safely required experience."

"I'll ask again. You have any idea who might have done it?"

"The Triads. I found a letter to my dad about a guy named C. B. Chen in Hong Kong. He bosses the overseas Triad gangs. He said Chen was capable of almost anything. And then there's W. Billy Caspar's group. And J. Ames. Ames left that threatening phone call after we closed down his ranch."

"You still have that tape?"

"I erased it by mistake."

"Too bad," said Metcalf. "You get any phone calls on the answering machine, keep 'em. Change the tape again if you have to. Would you recognize the voice?"

"Yes."

"I'll ask the Merced sheriffs about Ames. You think he kidnapped Dmitri for a ransom?" Metcalf asked.

"I don't know what to think."

Metcalf said, "Driving over here, I thought about what you would do with a tiger like Dmitri when he woke up. You'd have him in a cage, and then what?"

"You'd take the cage out of the truck and pull it into a building to hide him, or you'd keep the cage in the truck."

"I've heard him bellow. I'd think you'd have to be on a farm or a ranch, or someone would hear him."

"You can hear him from a long way off," Ben agreed.

"If the Chinese stole him, he's worth more dead than alive. Is that right?"

Ben didn't want to consider that, but it was true. "A lot more."

Metcalf nodded. "Ben, I investigate people crimes. This one is way out of my league. I'm going to need to call in some experts. So I want you to think about all the possibilities and call me later today. Meanwhile, I'll send the crime lab here."

Metcalf also thought they should phone the media. "They'll hear about it soon enough, and who knows, they might get a lead."

Then the deputy left Los Coyotes.

Graciela came up to the office, frowning. "Ben, Quan Li is gone. His trailer door is open. He's gone. Nothing of him is left. Nothing. His Honda is gone."

"You sure, Gracey?"

"I'm sure."

"Thanks for telling me."

Why would Quan Li leave so suddenly? He wasn't supposed to go to UC Davis for another three weeks. Was he involved?

Was Quan Li, in fact, a Triad? Did he help with the kidnapping? His father would laugh. "Quan Li? Quan Li? He's not capable of kidnapping a parakeet."

Ben wasn't so sure.

XXXI

RANSOM

Joking about having to come back so soon after the Ji Luk case, county crime technicians arrived to take photos of the tire tracks, make casts of them, and dust the front gate as well as Dimmy's gate for fingerprints. One said, "I'll track down your tiger if you'll trade him for my mother-in-law. She belongs in a cage." Ben didn't laugh.

Now he was unhappily answering media phone calls. Most of the reporters sounded skeptical or amused. Was it a publicity stunt? Los Coyotes was getting more press than the White House.

"Who would kidnap a big tiger?"

Ben had no answer to give.

"You sure you didn't let it loose on purpose?"

A silly question. "No way. Very sure."

"Is it insured?"

"No." His father had tried Lloyd's of London, and even they wouldn't insure Dmitri.

"Have you had a ransom demand?"

"No."

"How did they get him out of there?"

"Knocked him out and transferred him to a cage in a truck." That was an educated guess, but as good as any.

"Was everyone asleep?"

"Yes." He knew that made him and the staff sound like genuine, dumbhead klutzes.

Ben referred the reporters to Susan for any other questions, knowing the press would have laughs with the story, play games with it.

TV already had a lot of stock footage on Dmitri, including shots of him hurling the long-handled shovels over the fence, but the networks still sent out camera crews to photograph empty Compound Number One. Ben thought that was silly.

"Whom do you suspect?" Susan wanted to know.

He told her what he'd already told Deputy Metcalf. Ames or the Triads were his choices. Ames had nothing to lose; he'd collect the ransom and sell the carcass to the Chinese.

A few minutes later, Metcalf called. "I'm getting a lot of heat from my boss about wasting our assets on an animal."

The same thing had happened with the sniper incident. Metcalf had handled that by saying that if a human was killed, not an animal, the department would have to take the responsibility. His boss shut up. This time it was different. There was no sniper with a deadly weapon this time.

"I'm not sure who has the ball here. Maybe Animal Control?" Metcalf said.

Frank Coffey? Ben couldn't think of anyone worse.

"Mr. Metcalf, this took a lot of planning. The kind of planning only a very serious organization can do. Probably a crime organization. It's not like stealing a pet pony. At least one experienced big-cat handler had to be involved, someone who knew the right dosage to knock out Dimmy, not kill him."

"That sounds reasonable," Metcalf said. "But Ben, these animal cases are tricky. We've had stolen prize cats, stolen prize dogs, stolen prize horses. They can turn into legal nightmares if they get to court. Yours is different. That tiger is supposed to be a killer, a threat to the public if he gets loose. And even if he isn't a killer, just the thought of him scares me."

"Well, if he is a threat to people, then it's a job for you and not Coffey, right?" Ben asked.

"Good point."

"I have an idea that whoever has him did research," Ben added. "My father made a mistake by telling the press that the circus offered us a half million for him."

"Whoever's got him may double that," Metcalf said. "They sure aren't going to return him. They'll probably leave him in that cage somewhere in the boondocks if you pay the ransom."

"You think we'll have to do that?"

"You may, if you want him back alive. But let's hope we can find him before you turn over the cash."

"What do I do?" Ben asked.

"Wait until whoever has him gets in touch with you. Call me the minute it happens."

Ben didn't waste precious time trying to figure out exactly how they'd swiped Dimmy. Instead he concentrated on what he knew about transporting big cats. Where did they get the cage? A cage could be bought or rented. Zoo-supply outfits were all around the country. Call zoo-supply people? Any big rental truck with a drop ramp could have been used to load the cage with Dimmy inside it. Call rental companies?

Rolling along a back country road or a freeway, it wasn't likely Dimmy would roar. Stopped, he might let out a nervous bellow.

Less than an hour later, the fax machine rang, and the message began sliding through: *To whoever is in charge of Los Coyotes Preserve, we have your Siberian tiger. He's in good shape and will stay that way if you do exactly what we say. We will inform you where he can be located on receipt of $500,000 cash. We understand that it will take time to raise that amount of money. Therefore we will give you 72 hours to do so. On expiration of that time period, he will be killed. In 15 minutes you will receive a phone call. Answer it on the third ring by saying yes or no. We will fax the next step within six hours.*

Ben was watching the fax as it came out of the back of the Panasonic. He noticed that it had no identification. There was no way to trace it.

He looked up at the office clock. The time was 2:00 P.M., and the date was September 5. They had until 2:00 P.M. on September 8. His dad would pay the money for Dimmy, he was certain.

He called Susan and read it to her. She said, "I'm not surprised."

He called Metcalf. The deputy said to answer yes. "Play for time. We've got a lot to do, and not much time to do it." He reeled off instructions, including, "Tell the press about the ransom figure."

The phone rang in fifteen minutes, and Ben said one word: "Yes."

The next call came from Susan about an hour later. "Ben, I've polled all the board members, and each one, even Larry Templeton, said that Dmitri isn't worth paying the ransom. I'm sorry, but I agree. This is a business matter, preserve money."

Ben's stomach turned over. He couldn't even talk to Susan and got off the phone. How could they think this way? Ben sat in the chair by Whitney's desk, fighting back tears.

Jilly and Whitney came back from the crime scene a few minutes later. Finally, he said to them, "The board won't put up the five hundred thousand. We've got to find Dimmy before the seventy-two hours are up."

"Do you think those people are serious?" Jilly asked.

"They're serious."

Ben dialed Deedee. Before he could even ask her, his grandmother said she'd heard from Susan. "Ben, I know how much that tiger means to you, but I voted against paying the kidnappers. It's simply too much money."

"People come from everywhere on Sunday afternoons to see him. He earns all that money for us and the Russian biosphere. Whoever has him knows that."

"You may be right," she said, but she offered no help. The tone of her voice was flat.

"He could die," Ben insisted. "They can get something out of him that way. They can sell his carcass for a lot of money to the Chinese."

"Susan said they may be bluffing. She said she'll try to find a way to counter offer. Maybe they'll accept half of what they want?"

Ben said, "We don't have much time."

Deedee couldn't resist saying, "Ben, now you know what it means to run the preserve. You should be out enjoying yourself and not be involved in this mess."

"Enjoying himself" was not a priority right now. "The only person really helping me is Deputy Metcalf," he snapped, and he hung up the phone.

Now that the board, including his own grand-mother, had walked away, he was totally alone. Ben left the office and headed for the compounds, trying to think of what else he could do.

Ben knew that Alfredo was checking a new ship-ment of raw meat that had just come in. He went down to the freezer to tell Alfredo about the ransom money and that the board had decided not to pay it; even his grandmother had agreed. "What do we do?" Ben asked.

Alfredo blew out a breath and shook his head. "I don't know. Gracey would probably say, 'Pray for a miracle.' She might be right, Ben."

"I feel so helpless," Ben was telling him as Whitney's voice came over the preserve loudspeaker:

"Ben, Deputy Metcalf wants you to call him. . . ." He headed back to the office.

By the time he got back to the cottage, Metcalf had left for a court appearance, and it wasn't until after 5:30 that he finally reached Ben.

"I called the Dean of Graduate Studies at UC Davis this morning. He'd never heard of Quan Li; no application was filed from Taiwan for anyone named Quan Li. I took it further and faxed the University of Taiwan, in Taipei. They haven't had a student named Quan Li since 1965. If that is the case, Mr. Quan Li has to be forty-some years old, not twenty-nine. I think you boarded a Triad, and your boarder may have Dmitri."

"I can't believe that," Ben said.

"That's how it goes sometimes with con men," Metcalf said. "Sorry."

After hanging up, Ben thought about the two days Quan Li had spent watching Dmitri; about the mysterious shorting of the alarm systems. Why didn't his father check Quan Li's credentials more closely?

How could any of this be happening?

DEPUTY JARVIS

Ben was stunned by the deputy's news about Quan Li. The student had seemed so quiet, not someone Ben could imagine mixed up with Triads, or any organized crime. It didn't seem possible that Quan Li could have been involved with the kidnapping. Yet how else could Metcalf explain his background check?

Besides the Triads, the only other likely suspect would have to be Ames. He and Caspar had made direct threats against Los Coyotes, and Ames might even have the knowledge to safely tranquilize big cats. Both men were active members of United Sportsmen.

Wilder still, could Quan Li be, in any way, associated with Ames? Split the money with Ames? That was unlikely, Ben thought, but everything that had happened so far had been unlikely.

Ben decided to call Deputy Jarvis, Merced County sheriff's department.

"This is Ben Jepson, Mr. Jarvis. You may remember me. My friend Jilly Coombes and I got into trouble at the Ames hunt ranch over trespassing. We came up from Orange County."

Jarvis said, "Yeah, I remember you." His voice was not warm.

Ben quickly told him that Dmitri had been kidnapped, and a half-million-dollar ransom had been demanded. Ben also told him about the Ames threat.

Jarvis warmed up.

"Do you know where Ames is now?" Ben asked him.

"Have no idea," Jarvis said. "But I do know that the Fish and Game wardens shut him down with our help. I wasn't assigned to the raid. They call us when they think there may be a problem. Ames had a lot of guns out there, I heard. It was coordinated by Sacramento."

Ben knew all that.

"You might call them. I remember reading in the local paper that Ames sold his animals to a canned-hunt ranch in Montana. Hauled them away in several cattle trucks. Then I saw something about his property being up for sale for a million. You and that other kid caused him a lot of grief. I told you about his criminal record. I warned you not to mess with him."

Ben said, "I guess we did cause him trouble." And this was Ames's payback time.

"Not much to guess about."

"I think he might have kidnapped Dmitri," Ben said.

"Hey, that's dangerous talk, unless you can prove it. I'd be careful who you tell that to, especially any press people."

"I'm only telling you."

"I didn't hear what you said," Jarvis said carefully.

"I understand."

"I'll ask around about Ames's whereabouts, but let your local authorities deal with it. You're too young to get involved."

Ben thanked him and called Metcalf and Susan to repeat what Jarvis had told him. He left out the part about not being involved. No one was already involved more than he was. That's the way it would stay until they got Dimmy back.

Four hours into the allotted seventy-two hours, the fax machine awakened with another message: *You will be asked to place unmarked $100 bills in the amount of $500,000 in a locked suitcase and stand by for further directions.*

Susan said, "Well, they're for real, but we still won't pay it."

The office clock was getting to Ben. Time was speeding by. He asked Luis if he had any idea where Salvadore Sanchez, the Ames ranch worker who'd called about the Bengal, might be.

Luis said he'd make some calls. Ben knew that the Latinos, wherever they were, often kept in touch. Their communities, especially in farm areas, were close-knit. Someone might know where Salvadore Sanchez was working now. Ben understood some Spanish as Luis made call after call.

Several calls later, Luis's eyes lit up. "*Suceso!*" he

said. "I found him. He's working on a ranch near Le Grand, south of Planada."

"Have someone get to him, and ask him to call us collect," Ben told Luis. "Tell them it's an emergency."

More rapid-fire talk by Luis, then he looked at Ben and said, "We wait."

An hour later, the phone rang. Salvadore Sanchez!

Ben said, "Ask him if he knows where Ames is. Ask if he's seen him lately." Ben crossed his fingers.

The back-and-forth in Spanish was under way. Finally, Luis said, "He saw him driving his pickup on Route 140 about two weeks ago. . . ."

"Have Sanchez give us a phone number where we can reach him."

Luis nodded.

Ben now had the strongest hunch that Dimmy was in Merced County and maybe not far from where Ames had operated. *What next? What do I do next?* It was 10:10. Every time the clock hands rotated was a minute lost. He said to Luis, "Let's get everyone together. Wake 'em up if necessary."

Luis went out.

———

One by one, they filed in, Alfredo in his pajamas; Ricky in bare feet; sleepy-eyed Odinga; Rafael in a sweatshirt; Whitney in overalls.

They all knew about Ames. Ben didn't have to waste words. "We found out tonight that Ames is still hanging around Planada, and I think he may have something to do with kidnapping Dimmy. I don't have any proof, just a gut hunch. I also think he might have Dimmy hidden away, hoping we'll pay the ransom."

"Have you told that to the police up there?" Odinga asked.

"I talked to the sheriff's office this morning, but I know they won't begin searching for a tiger unless someone spots him."

Whitney said, "How about posters in the Latino markets?"

"We don't have time for that."

Luis said, "The best eyes and ears are the farm and ranch workers. They're like a secret underground."

"How do we get to them in a hurry?"

Luis broke out in a wide grin. "*Cantinas*, of course. Tomorrow night is Saturday night, and they'll gather in the *cantinas* to drink *cerveza* and dance to our country music." Word of mouth, the best communication of all.

Odinga said, "Why not offer a reward?"

"Yes." Alfredo nodded.

Luis said, agreeing, "Whisper in their ears, tell them not to tell the *gringos* but say they can make some good money. Poor *campesinos* will listen. One may already know. They are not ignorant, just divided by language."

"I'll get the money," Ben said, "and we'll go up there tomorrow." He thanked them all and went to the phone.

Grammy Deedee usually read in bed until 11:00. She had told Ben to call her anytime, night or day, if he needed her. It was 10:45, and he needed her.

She answered on the first ring. Ben explained that Dimmy might be in Merced Country; that Ben wanted to offer a reward of ten thousand dollars for any information leading to the arrest of individuals involved in the kidnapping. He'd thought about five thousand at first, but then decided to make it rich enough to create solid interest. Could he borrow ten thousand?

Deedee was silent for at least a minute. Then she said, "Ben, I have a deal for you."

Oh, man, he knew what was coming. Any deal from Deedee or his mother had to do with education.

She said, "I'll write you a check for ten thousand if you agree to return to school next week. Further, you'll have to agree to college and graduate. I'll put all this in writing tomorrow."

"Deedee, you know how much I hate school."

"I do. I also know how much you need it."

"This isn't fair. How about just lending me the ten thousand?"

"I'm not a bank, Ben."

Defeated, Ben sighed.

"I'm deaf, Ben. Do we have a deal?"

Everything he stood for was about to go down the chute if he didn't agree.

"Yes," he said reluctantly.

"Good night, Ben," she said.

When you are young, it's hell to be taken advantage of, Ben thought.

His last call that night was to Jilly Coombes. "Jilly, I need your help one last time."

"No way," Jilly told him. Jilly had pulled a muscle

in practice and couldn't play the nonleague opener Saturday night, but he wasn't about to miss seeing the game.

"Please, Jilly. Please! I need you, man."

"For what?"

"We have to go back up to Merced County."

"*We?*"

"We'd be looking for Dimmy and maybe Ames," Ben said.

"No way," Jilly said again. "We got in big trouble last time."

"You've got to help." Jilly knew about the seventy-two-hour deadline. "Dimmy could be killed." Ben explained about offering the reward, getting the message out to Mexican field-workers.

"How do you come up with all this stuff?"

"I didn't. Luis told me about Saturday nights in the *cantinas*. Odinga came up with the reward idea. I just listen, Jilly."

"Am I going to drive your mother's car?"

"No, we'll take yours. The BMW is too fancy to be running around in the boondocks up there."

"Ben, some of those farm owners have Cadillacs."

"The VW," Ben insisted.

"Suppose Ames spots me?"

"Okay, okay. You'll drive the BMW. We'll leave here at 6:30. You and me and Luis."

Ben woke up Luis, told him the departure time, and then went out to the BMW and put the Colt under the front passenger seat. He didn't want to forget it.

Returning to the cottage, he went straight to bed, knowing he wouldn't sleep much.

Sixty hours of the deadline time was left, ticking away, until whoever had Dmitri might kill him.

XXXIII
MOTEL EIGHT

Jilly arrived not long after sunrise, fifty-five hours before deadline. Jilly was carrying a paper bag and slid it under the driver's seat.

"What was that?" Ben asked.

"My dad's .38."

Luis Vargas overhead him and said flatly, "I'm not going!"

Ben turned toward Luis. "Why not?"

"You think I'm *loco*, Ben? You carry a concealed weapon, and we get stopped. Teenager driving a

BMW, you next to him, adult Latino in the back-seat?" He shook his head. "No way!"

Concealed weapon. Ben hadn't thought about that. "That was nutty," he admitted. *Two kids with concealed guns. Hadn't given it a thought.*

Opening the passenger door, he retrieved his Colt from under his seat and then walked around the car to get the .38 in Jilly's bag. He took them both into the office.

When Ben got back in the car, Luis said, "I don't want even a sniff of pot or a beer can in this car."

Ben said meekly, "We're both clean."

Alfredo was there in his bathrobe with Odinga to see them off and wish them luck.

Whitney had come in early to give him $300 out of petty cash. He had the corporate Visa card.

Luis got into the backseat of the BMW, and they headed north on 99 for Planada. He soon went to sleep.

Ben kept looking at his watch. His mouth was already dry, and his stomach ached. He found it hard to talk. The BMW could cruise easily at seventy-five, and every time he saw Jilly dropping below that number, he said, "Come on, man. We need to get to Planada."

Jilly said, "You remember that Ames had all those rifles in his office."

"I remember."

"I don't think he'd hesitate to use one."

"I told you Fish and Game shut him down, and I have the phone number of the sheriffs in Merced. The minute we find Dmitri, if we find him, I'll call Jarvis."

"You better."

Two hours later, Ben glanced into the mirror and saw flashing red lights behind them. "There's a black and white on our tail," he said to Jilly. The speedometer read eighty-five. Thank the Lord and Luis that they'd left the guns at home.

Jilly cursed, slowing down, finally pulling off to the shoulder. He shook his head at Ben. "Great."

The patrolman went through the usual police routine with a little more thoroughness than usual. He made all three leave the car. He ordered Jilly to open the trunk. Ben showed him the registration after he checked Jilly's driver's license. Then he wrote out the ticket, warned Jilly to ease up on the pedal, and waved them good-bye. They'd lost a half hour.

Ben said, "I'll pay the fine!"

Jilly was burning. "Will you also go to traffic school?"

Ben called Whitney from a gas station. "Any other message from them?" *The kidnappers, of course.*

"None."

They checked into a Motel Eight on the outskirts of Planada in midafternoon, seven hours since they left the preserve. As they'd turned onto 140, Ben saw a sheriff's substation at the intersection of Sutter Street and the highway, and he made a mental note to look up the phone number in case they needed a deputy in a hurry. Merced Township was eight or ten miles west.

Ben called Whitney again to let her know where they were, gave her the phone number, and asked her to spend the night at the preserve just in case there was another fax.

Ninety percent of the faces in Planada were brown. It was in the heart of grape, cotton, almond, walnut, corn, and pear country. Farming and cattle-growing, east up the road where Ames had his ranch, were the only occupations.

They drove to Merced to do business with an

instant printer. Luis wanted business cards in Spanish announcing the reward. The cards said to call them at the motel number if anyone had information about the tiger.

Headed west again on 140 toward Planada, Ben said, "Let's go take a look at Ames's place." He didn't think Ames would be foolish enough to park Dimmy at the Morning Glory, but it wouldn't hurt to take a look.

There was a FOR SALE sign on the fence of the Morning Glory, but no vehicles around it. The front gate was chained. No lights on inside the office. No horses in the corral. Ames wasn't at home, but Ben still felt the danger of his presence.

The cropland extended beyond Planada for a few miles, and then low, grassy autumn-brown hills, dotted with oaks, marked the beginning of cattle ranches, stretching to Mariposa. Yosemite and the Sierra Nevada range climbed into the sky a little to the northeast, blue-green in the distance.

At twilight, Luis said, "It all looks so beautiful and peaceful, but there are meth labs all over the place. This is big-money druggie heaven."

Ben was even more tense now that they had seen

Ames's old place. "Guys," he said, "we've got less than forty-eight hours to find Dimmy." Beauty and peace weren't on his mind, nor were meth labs.

Cantina Dos Hermanos, the Two Brothers beer joint, was located about two miles east of town. It was smoky and crowded by eight o'clock on Saturday night, the dance floor packed with dreamy-eyed waltzers. A five-piece band — electric guitar, violin, trumpet, accordion, and drums — serenaded the dancers. The rich colors of Mexico, reds and greens, were everywhere. Neon blue ringed the bar.

Some of the men wore cowboy boots, silk shirts, and shiny dark pants; others were dressed in white shirts and jeans. Some of the women wore long gowns. They sat at tables. Others were at the bar. Over in a corner were mothers and children, some asleep. After the week of hard work in the fields, this was their night for fun.

There wasn't a *gringo* in the room aside from Jilly and Ben, but that was all right, Luis said. Anyway, they were with him.

Luis sized up the room and finally said, "Time for me to go to work." He got up and went to the table nearest them. He sat down with the two couples there. They appeared to be listening intently as he talked about kidnapped Dmitri and the reward, handing over the business card.

Then he went on to another table. The word would spread quickly, Ben hoped. Ten thousand was a lot of money.

They stayed there more than an hour and then went on to another four *cantinas*. Midnight went by, and at about 1:30, when the last *cantina* closed, they went back to Motel Eight.

"How many people know?" Ben asked Luis.

"A lot, Ben. A whole lot."

"What now?" he asked.

"We wait for the phone to ring," Luis said. "There's nothing more we can do."

"Suppose it doesn't ring tonight?"

Luis's dark eyes said more than his double-word answer. "We wait."

Jilly and Ben roomed together. Ben wasn't sure he slept at all because of Jilly's snoring. And when the sun rose the next morning over the San Joaquin Valley, all he could think about was this: They had thirty-nine hours left to find Dimmy. In the distance a church bell rang for early Mass. Maybe he should go and pray that one of those business cards had gotten into the right hands.

Ben punched Jilly's shoulder and said he was going out and would bring back breakfast. He took the BMW keys off the night table. Jilly nodded and rolled over.

If Luis's phone had rung during the night, Ben knew he would have woken them. Ben had to face the fact that Dimmy might not be in the San Joaquin, or even in California. He could be in Montana by now, in Arizona or Texas, or even down in Baja Mexico.

Ben thought of Dmitri, helpless in some cage. Dmitri was utterly dependent upon humans for survival. He had been since Ben picked him up as a baby in the frozen taiga. He wouldn't understand why Ben wasn't with him. And now he was in danger of being slaughtered.

Ben found a café open and ordered breakfast burritos for three, orange juice, and coffee to go. It was going to be a very long day. They would watch football, play cards, and wait — as Luis had said.

JAVIER USABIAGA

Most of the day was pure torture. Luis couldn't leave the room because he was the only one who spoke Spanish, so they were holed up like a trio of bank robbers. Ben had gotten a deck of cards out of the motel office, and they began watching NFL football in midmorning. He constantly looked at the clock in Luis's room, silently begging the phone to ring.

Ben had called Whitney. Still no message as to where the ransom should be dropped. Metcalf had said the kidnappers would probably leave that until the last hour. Maybe a half-dozen times Ben asked, "Why doesn't somebody call?"

Luis was tired of hearing it. He said, "Go take a walk, Ben. The *campesinos* are talking about it, I know. Right now, someone is hearing about the reward who didn't know about it last night. There is nothing we can do except wait."

Easy for you to say, Ben thought. Yet when the radio clock turned to 2:00 p.m., they'd be exactly twenty-four hours away from the possibility of Dmitri being killed for whatever his carcass was worth. Maybe Dimmy was already dead?

Ben and Jilly went out to bring back sandwiches and drinks. He hated to think about it, but time was running out. "I guess we'll go home tomorrow after-noon unless we get a break."

"Come on, Ben, we've got most of the day left and all of the night. Didn't your father ever tell you to think positively? Mine does."

"Yes, he did." *All the time. The thought of his father made his whole body ache, but he was determined to push it out of his mind. This was not the time to be pulled under by thoughts that were almost too bleak to comprehend.*

When they got back to Motel Eight, Luis had a wide grin on his face. "The phone rang, Benjamin!" He showed Ben a slip of paper with the name *Javier Usabiaga* on it.

Ben almost kissed him.

"Javier walks to work every day by an abandoned packinghouse, one built in the 1940s. It hasn't been used in thirty years. He's always thought there were ghosts in there, and yesterday morning he thought he heard a muffled noise coming from it. He said it sounded like a roar. . . ."

Ben was scarcely breathing.

"When I asked him if the roar sounded like an animal, he said it did, a very big animal, like a lion. He ran like hell. . . ."

Heart pounding, Ben said, "Dmitri."

Luis nodded. "It could be. Javier is a picker and is overwhelmed to think he might get ten thousand from this. Only his family knows, and I told him not to tell anyone else. He agreed."

"Where is the packinghouse?"

"Up a road off 140. He gave me directions to where he lives, and we'll park there tonight and walk with him. If we can make sure Javier wasn't hearing ghosts, you can call your sheriff friend in Merced."

"Do you think this place would be big enough for Dmitri?"

"I remember one outside of Chowchilla," Luis told him, "an old one not far from where we lived growing up. There was a basement under it fifteen feet deep, and tons of ice would be dropped in down there; then fans would blow cool air over the vegetables. This was before refrigeration. It had three bays where the produce trucks would load. I'm not sure it's still there."

"Could you get a truck inside and then close the outer door?"

"Yes."

They had dinner and then went west on 140 to the turnoff for Javier's house, going north on that dirt road in the thick darkness. Two miles up a half-dozen picker houses stood, small and shabby in the head-light glow. Outside one, in hand-painted mailbox letters, Ben could see the name *Usabiaga*.

Luis got out and walked up to the door. It opened,

and in the dimness of the inside lights, Ben could see the slim figure of a man, likely Javier, as well as a woman and several children.

Luis talked, then Javier trailed him back to the car. Jilly and Ben got out and shook hands with Javier. He was thin-faced, skin mahogany-colored. His family remained in the doorway, looking out at them. Even at night, with shadows hiding the poverty, Ben could tell they had very little.

"Come," Luis said, and they followed Javier behind his house across crop fields for about a half mile, coyotes howling in the distance. Finally they stepped out on a hardtop road. They didn't say a word on the walk. A cool breeze was blowing, carrying an acrid fertilizer smell.

They turned south, toward 140, and after about fifteen minutes they saw the shadow of a large building on the right side of the road. Fifty feet away, Ben could see that the packinghouse was made of concrete blocks and corrugated sheet metal. Huge wooden doors stood at the four bay entrances. Creaking sounds came from loose pieces of metal, attacked by the wind. It was ghostly, probably day or night.

Luis and Javier talked in a whisper for a moment, and then Javier vanished into the night, heading home. Now that he'd led them there, he wanted nothing further to do with this.

As Ben, Luis, and Jilly moved closer to the rear of the oblong building, they could see a white pickup parked back there, not visible from the road. Going up to it cautiously, Ben felt the hood. It was cold. No one had started the engine for hours. The owner might be in the building. Ames, perhaps?

He whispered, "I'll go around to the front." The loading bays were there, and if Dimmy was in a truck, he might smell Ben.

There was litter all around, thirty years of it, and twice Ben tripped over pieces of board. But he kept on his feet, trying to see if there were tire tracks leading up to any of the bays.

His eyes had adjusted to the night and it was surprising just how much he could see. On the busted concrete driveway leading off the hardtop to Bay Four, he thought he saw recent tracks that crushed down weeds and debris. He got down on his hands and knees and confirmed them. A truck had driven in not long ago. Maybe two or three days.

He carefully made his way up to the door. There was a new padlock.

Pressing his face against the door crack, he saw a bright yellow truck. What was it doing in a packinghouse that hadn't operated in thirty years? There was not enough light, however, despite the roof cracks, to tell whether or not the moving van had a cage inside it. It was like looking into a cave. But then Ben smelled tiger. The odor of a tiger confined in a small space was always strong. Dimmy was in there; he was sure of it.

He backed away and soon joined Luis and Jilly.

He told them he'd seen a big truck in Bay Four, that the door had a shiny new padlock, that tire tracks led to the door, and that he smelled Dmitri.

"You're sure," Jilly said.

"Dimmy's in there."

Luis said, "Let's go."

They found their way back to Javier's house. Luis told him that what they were looking for was probably in the packinghouse. If so, a cashier's check for ten thousand would be in the mail for him within days. There were smiles and hand claps from all the Usabiagas.

It was late by the time they got back to Motel Eight. Ben put in a call to Metcalf. Thankfully, he was home.

"We found Dmitri. He's in a moving van at an old abandoned packinghouse up here off Route 140 in Merced County."

"Are you certain?"

"I couldn't see him, but I did see the truck. It's in one of the packinghouse bays. So what do I do now?"

"Be sure of what you're telling me, Ben. I don't want to get egg on my face."

"I'm sure of what I've told you, but I don't know if Dimmy is dead or alive. I couldn't see into the van. It was too dark in there. But I smelled him."

"All right, I'll call the Merced sheriff for you. Give me that motel number. If I can convince him, I imagine they'll go for it first thing in the morning."

Next call was to Alfredo. Ben told him what he'd told Metcalf.

"Thank God," Alfredo said. "I'll tell everyone here."

After a call from the night-duty sergeant in the Merced sheriff's office, confirming that they'd visit the derelict packinghouse on Cunningham Road at

7:00 in the morning, Ben, Jilly, and Luis went back to the first *cantina* to slow down — and to celebrate.

When they got back to the motel, Ben set the clock alarm for a 5:30 wake-up. But he didn't get much sleep. All night he worried that Dimmy might be dead.

SURPRISE

With the San Joaquin sun shining brightly, seven Merced sheriffs' cars, four marked, arrived on time at the rendezvous point, and Ben talked to the sergeant-in-charge, Mr. Curran. He was a square-faced man about fifty who looked like Tommy Lee Jones. Meanwhile, others gathered around. Ben told them everything that he'd told Metcalf and the duty sergeant the previous night.

Curran immediately dispatched a marked car to go a quarter mile beyond the packinghouse and stop all traffic. There were four POP (Problem-Oriented Policing) officers dressed in black, with helmets and armored vests. The other eleven deputies were in their usual greenish uniforms.

Ben was exhausted, but his eyes were bright. "I think we'll find the world's largest known tiger in that van. He weighs 800 pounds and is thirteen feet from the tip of his nose to his tail. He'll be contained within a steel cage. He may scare you, but please don't shoot him. Please don't. . . ."

"Are you listening?" Curran said to the deputies.

Frowning, one of the deputies said, "The tiger was actually kidnapped?"

"That is correct. Maybe the world's first kidnapped tiger. *Don't shoot it*," Curran ordered.

Looking at the faces, Ben could tell that the officers wondered why there was such a turnout of force just to rescue a circus animal. He was sure that's how they thought of Dimmy.

Curran cleared the air. "Some of you know who James Ames is. Some don't. He's a convicted felon with a criminal record. He did three years in San Quentin for assault with a deadly weapon. Shot a man in Madera. He got out of a meth-lab bust about five years ago. He's suspected of ransoming this animal for a half million. He threatened this young man with a shotgun. He may be inside there. Do I need to tell you more?"

No, he didn't.

Curran turned back to Ben. "You can follow us, but stay out of the way." Ben nodded.

The raid party parked diagonally in front of the four bays, the POP officers getting out of their car with automatic-fire rifles. All the others, except Curran, drew pistols, and Ben pointed to Number Four Bay.

One deputy went back to his car for a bolt cutter and eased up to the twin doors. They looked to be twelve to fifteen feet high. The padlock fell, and he wrenched the old doors wide open, letting the strong sun in, getting a five-mile roar from an outraged Dmitri, who was framed in the cage bars. The sound was like a hoarse blast of a dozen ships blowing at once.

Dimmy's face was contorted, canines appearing six inches long, the brown-gold eyes turned to solid gold. The roars, bellowing straight from his gut, echoed through the ancient building.

There were frightened shouts from the deputies. Three of them fell on their backs from pure shock. Mouths sagging open, they were frozen, staring at Dmitri in awe. *He was Lord of the Kill.*

Ben had heard him roar thousands of times before, but never like this. Insanity was in his throat. Ben knew why: All his life, Dmitri had lived in the freedom and fresh air of his four acres. He'd always been fed regularly. Now he'd been confined in dark, alien silence for at least forty-eight hours; he'd smelled the tub of raw meat packed in ice not ten feet away. He was starved. *He was a truly wild animal now.* Humans had done this to him, and Dimmy would remember the trauma until he died.

Luis's face had turned ashen white. Jilly stood there like a zombie.

"I'm going in," said Ben.

Curran shouted at Ben, "Is it safe to go in there?"

Ben could see that the cage, with its three-quarter-inch steel bars, was padlocked. Dimmy would need a hacksaw or acetylene torch to get out. "Yeah," he shouted.

He ran to the tub, yelling for Luis and Jilly to help him. He pulled handfuls of the meat out of the ice and stood on his tiptoes to shove it onto the cage floor, risking his fingers as Dimmy scooped it up. The roars had dropped to angry machine-gun muttering. No one could have gone into that cage and come out alive. They gave him at least twenty pounds of meat to quell the starvation. They'd give him more later.

The deputies, still holding their firearms, cautiously entered the bay and inspected the Acme rental truck. One climbed up to the cab and yelled, "Sergeant, we got another problem up here."

Curran moved quickly, hopped up on the running board, and looked in over the deputy's shoulder. "Someone call the office. We need our homicide men here," he yelled. "Guy's dead in the front seat. Looks like he's been shot. We'll need the coroner."

Ben couldn't believe what he heard. It didn't seem possible that his trip to the Morning Glory Ranch to check on a Bengal would end up in another murder.

Curran yelled again. "Don't touch anything! Look where you step! This is now a homicide scene, fellows, so let's help the investigators. Forget about the tiger. We don't have any more interest in him."

Ben took the car and went off to call Alfredo from

a phone booth. "We have Dimmy," he said. "He's okay, but he was hungry. He scared all these deputy sheriffs and me half to death. Get the squeeze cage and put it in the CAT WAGN and come up here as fast as you can. Come up 99 to Plainsburg Road, take a right to Planada, and then east on 140 to . . ."

"Hey, not so fast," Alfredo said. "I'm writing this down."

". . . to Cunningham Road, four or five miles east of Planada, turn left, and you'll see the old packing-house about two miles up. Have Odinga fix two doses of phencyclidine and atropine. We'll need Odinga here. We have to tranquilize Dimmy to get him out of that cage."

"Gotcha."

"Now for the shocker. The sheriffs found a dead body in the moving van. The guy was shot."

"Good Lord. Who got killed?"

"I have no idea. Tell everyone Dimmy is okay; tell them we'll start back as soon as you get here. Probably have to spend the night somewhere up here. Have Whitney call my grandmother and Susan."

Ben returned to the packinghouse and said to Jilly,

"I'm going to wait for Odinga and Alfredo. You can go on home if you want."

Jilly said, "No way. I want to stick around for all the fun."

The ambulance and the medical examiner soon arrived, along with the usual homicide unit, a photographer, and the county crime lab. Dimmy had partially settled down and was licking his paws.

Just inside the bay doorway, out of the sun, was a gurney with a body laid out on a red plastic pad. Dried blood covered the white polyester jacket the victim was wearing. Dried blood left a path from the corner of his mouth down his throat. The bullet hole was in his forehead.

The man's dark brown eyes hadn't been closed, and his mouth hung open. There was a look of surprise on his face.

Ben stared at the white whiskerless skin and noticed the brown mole over the man's eyebrow. His voice shaking with disbelief, he said, "This isn't Ames. This man is W. Billy Caspar, president of United Sportsmen, a canned-hunt organization."

Sergeant Curran, standing nearby, said, "You know this guy, Ben?"

"I've seen him before. I heard him threaten my father at a congressional hearing in Washington. He and my dad were deadly enemies."

"Did Caspar have any connection to Mr. Ames?"

"Absolutely. My dad had some information on Caspar in his files."

Curran said, "Send it up to me." He handed Ben his card.

"Thank you for helping to rescue Dmitri," Ben said simply. Then he walked over to the other deputies, thanking as many of them as he could find.

Jilly was looking down at the corpse when Ben finally pulled him away. "Let's go into town for some food and drinks. Alfredo won't be up here until late afternoon or early evening."

At the restaurant, Ben called Metcalf to report what had happened, including Caspar's death. "Maybe the trouble is finally over. I hope so."

"So do I, Ben. You haven't had any recent trouble at the preserve aside from Dmitri, have you?"

"No."

"Any word from your parents?"

"No."

"I'm sorry about that. And there's still so much to do."

Metcalf added, "From where I sit, this case still isn't very pretty. I have to wade in the messes left behind by the canned-hunt people, the Triads, and victims like Ji Luk. Sometimes it all works out, but not always. There's an FBI statistic that more than 82 percent of all crimes are unreported or unsolved. I have to live with that. But you don't. Come home and restart your own life, Ben."

"I'll try, Mr. Metcalf."

"That's all you can do."

Luis, Ben, and Jilly sat in the shade of the packing-house for most of the afternoon until Alfredo and Odinga arrived. The law people came and went, working the crime scene. Ben had no desire to go back inside until it was time to roll the cage on the moving-van lift and transfer Dmitri to the CAT WAGN.

Luis and Jilly fell asleep for a while.

With his back against the warm concrete building, looking out over the crop fields up toward the Sierras, Ben did a lot of thinking that pretty September afternoon with autumn in the air.

He was worn out, dead tired, not the cocky Ben Jepson of the past. He realized now that he had been in way over his head even before his parents were reported missing. He was trying to be a boss when he wasn't ready for it. Although he'd done pretty well running Los Coyotes while they were away, it was no job for a six-teen-year-old. And sooner or later he'd blow something big time. He'd get someone hurt or killed. Jilly? The handlers? Himself?

Although he wasn't wild about the idea, he needed to go back to high school and then go to college, and finish it; get a degree. But he'd never be a nerd. Even Deedee wouldn't want that, he knew. He'd work at Los Coyotes when he wasn't in a classroom or grit-ting his teeth over books.

He'd think of his parents every single day, still convinced that they were alive. They would escape from whomever was holding them. "Ben, it's us. . . ."

He finally got up and went back inside the packinghouse to be near Dmitri. The tiger was asleep, likely having been awake for most of three days. The trauma had drained him, Ben thought. Ben would be there when Dimmy opened his eyes. He'd say, "How yuh doin', big fellow?"

Alfredo and Odinga arrived in late afternoon, and the cage was rolled onto the moving-van lift. Odinga then tranquilized Dmitri, and they slid him into the CAT WAGN for the long ride home.

Arriving back at the preserve, Whitney handed Ben a list of calls. Most were from the press, seeking information about Dmitri. "I think the urgent one is from Colonel Singh," she said. "He called yesterday."

"Get him for me, if you can, and page me on the loudspeaker."

Meanwhile, Ben went down to Number One where the CAT WAGN was parked at Dmitri's gate. Dimmy was still looking out at his four acres. Alfredo, Odinga, Luis, and Rafael were there. Ben said, "Let's do it," and he opened the gate. Luis backed up the wagon, and Ben opened the CAT WAGN door. Dimmy leapt a foot and was back inside Number One. He seemed happy to be there.

Ben returned to the office, exhausted. "I'm going to flake out," he said. "Wake me as soon as you get Gordie Singh."

Almost forty minutes passed until Whitney woke him up.

Singh was on the phone. "The kidnapped-tiger story played big over here. Anything to do with tigers does. You got him back safe and sound, huh?"

"Yes we did, Colonel."

"Congratulations! But that's not why I called. Ben, we've had at least nine sightings of your father and mother since that fifty-thousand-dollar reward was announced by *National Geographic*. The police are investigating each one. We think at least two of them are authentic. So I'm encouraged, and I hope you are, too. Two weeks ago, I wouldn't have given them a chance. But now, to be honest, I think they're alive. We have sources that say they were held against their will for a period of time. We know it had something to do with the Triads. Because of the international implications, the police don't care to discuss the circumstances, but they have strong reasons to believe your parents are alive. You must join them in that belief."

Ben sat down. The strength had run out of his legs. "I'll join them. Maybe my grandmother would want to double that reward."

"It wouldn't hurt," said Gordie Singh. "You take care."

NINA ZELENSKAYA
XXXVI

Five mornings after General Dmitri Zukov was returned to Los Coyotes, Ben invited all the staff plus Jilly, Templeton, Deedee, Susan Trager, and the Carpenters to an event to be held in Compound Number One.

He wasn't at all sure of the outcome, so he had both Luis and Rafael standing by with two supersized fire extinguishers, the type always used on "moving day."

When the group was gathered at about ten o'clock, Ben took a lead and walked up to Number Seven, the home of four Siberian tigresses. He entered it and called out to Nina Zelenskaya, a sleek and beautiful and sexy lady of five years, 406 pounds at the last weigh-in.

Nina had never caused a moment of trouble. She was a laid-back animal often used for photography with tour guests who looked straight into the camera, the visitor barely a foot from her, mustering a nervous smile. The unforgettable photo cost seventy-five dollars.

Putting the lead around her neck, Ben said, "I have a very special mission for you, Nina. I'm counting on you to help me." She responded with a *f-fouf*.

He led her out through the gate, locked it behind him, and said, "You've seen and heard Dmitri. He's just had a very traumatic experience, and I'm hoping you will be a warm and loving companion to him. He's never had a romance; never had his back or head groomed; never lived with a cat such as you."

Nina walked near to Ben's knees, her head up as if understanding every word.

Ben said, "I'm not sure what he'll do when I open his gate and let you in. But I promise I won't let you get hurt."

The humans outside Number One knew better than to talk as Ben and Nina approached. They also knew that Ben's father had always resisted the idea of bringing in a female to the "killer" star of Los Coyotes.

Ben's heart was pounding as he drew closer to Dimmy's gate. He motioned to Luis and Rafael to station themselves on either side of the gate. They lifted the big extinguishers in readiness.

Ben keyed the lock and opened the gate. Simultaneously he lifted the lead loop from Nina's neck. She stood motionless, looking at Dimmy. And he looked at her, for what seemed forever.

She was not in heat, Odinga had said, but as a special precaution, they'd given her a birth control pill the previous morning.

Finally, Nina Zelenskaya took a tentative step inside Dimmy's home and then another, moving toward him a few inches at a time.

Ben held the gate open a crack in case they had to rush in and rescue her. He was holding his breath. So were the other onlookers. He said to himself, *Go to him, Nina.*

Dimmy, up on all fours, seemed to be frozen in place, no other *Panthera* having ever entered his kingdom. The ambient gold eyes seemed enlarged. His breathing was slow and steady, every muscle alert.

If he were going to attack Nina, not knowing why she was there, it would be soon, Ben sensed. She was barely twenty feet from him.

The sight of the two tigers, both concentrating on each other, was one that his mother would have made into a masterpiece. It was a portrait of sheer beauty, one of those animal stories impossible to put into words. He knew his father would have wept.

Another two minutes passed, and Nina Zelenskaya reached Dimmy, responding to her femaleness of untold thousands of years, then used her tongue to lick the side of his head.

EPILOGUE

The next day, Ben reentered El Toro High to start his senior year. He planned to hire a tutor to help him with math and science. But he also continued to work afternoons and weekends at Los Coyotes.

He also applied to Saddleback Community College, ten miles away, to go after he graduated from El Toro. Deedee wasn't happy with his choice of colleges. Saddleback wasn't Yale or Harvard. But it was a start, and he'd eventually get a degree — he had promised.

The longtime preserve accountant, Phil Altman,

who had a degree in business administration, was hired to be temporary boss, while Alfredo and Odinga would share overseeing the big cats, with Ben participating on a spare-time basis. That was fine with Ben, even a relief. The board made the decision. Ben was no longer threatened with losing his bed in the cottage to a new director. And he was hopeful about his parents. Very hopeful. His father and mother had been facing danger their entire lives. The news was in their favor.

Another good thing was that Amos Carpenter overheard a retired dentist in the Golden Years saying he had paid Frank Coffey five thousand to get rid of the big cats. Frank had strung the "killer" sign up on the perimeter fence. When Animal Control found out, Frank was fired by the county.

One late afternoon in October, Metcalf phoned to say that the Merced County sheriff had called him. "Got some news for you. Once Ames had his canned-hunt business shut down, he started making meth again and apparently was taking too much of his own product. That stuff can drive you crazy. He talked Caspar into joining him to snatch your tiger, then killed him after an argument. He had connections with the Triads, but the connections aren't clear. We know a lot of money was involved. He'll be going to trial next year on a manslaughter charge. My guess is life — three strikes, and you're out."

"That is good news," Ben said. "How about Quan Li? You hear anything about him?"

"He remains the mysterious Mr. Li. They're certain he had something to do with the Triads and that hooker. But I'll tell you something, Ben, they couldn't give a hoot if they never find out. That's the way the real law works, not like TV. Don't dig badgers out of holes unless you have to."

Ben laughed. *Badgers! Quan Li?*

"Keep it cool out there," the deputy said.

"I'll try."

Ben sat a moment, just thinking about Number Twelve and the morning all the madness began. So much had happened since then. He looked at the clock and went to join Alfredo, Luis, Rafael, and Ricky at the chopping and feeding block. It was White Bucket Time.

He passed General Dmitri Zukov and Nina Zelenskaya on the way. They looked quite content.

AUTHOR'S NOTE

In 1984, I spent the better part of a year researching a book entitled *The Cats of Shambala*, about the life and times of actress Tippi Hedren and her big-cat compounds located in veldt-like terrain northeast of Los Angeles. It was an enchanted year, allowing me to enter the steel-fenced homes of lions, Bengal and Siberian tigers, leopards, cougars, and cheetahs, day and night; to meet and stroke *some* of the more amiable cats.

Just to walk around the compounds in total darkness, green eyes following my every footstep, was an unforgettable thrill. At Shambala, I learned the plight of the magnificent Siberian tigers in Russia and China, almost erased from earth by poachers to supply body parts to be ground into powder for the Asian medicinal trades. I knew that someday I'd write about this bloody tragedy.

In about 1991, deep-sea fishing off California's Dana Point for shark (to be caught and released), my longtime buddy, Ray Johnson, a longtime hunter, told me about *canned hunts*. I'd never heard of them and was shocked. The idea of zoos selling exotic animals to farmers and ranchers to be hunted down, slaughtered, and skinned for game-room trophies, was sickening. Big brave hunters killing bears in cages.

I decided to combine these two sordid stories, and *Lord of the Kill* is the result. I had much help in the writing from game wardens and the Humane Society.